Burns and Oates

Passing Away

Being some account of the last illness of my adopted child

Burns and Oates

Passing Away
Being some account of the last illness of my adopted child

ISBN/EAN: 9783742864789

Manufactured in Europe, USA, Canada, Australia, Japa

Cover: Foto ©Raphael Reischuk / pixelio.de

Manufactured and distributed by brebook publishing software
(www.brebook.com)

Burns and Oates

Passing Away

PASSING AWAY:

BEING

SOME ACCOUNT OF THE LAST ILLNESS
OF MY ADOPTED CHILD.

"We have loved her during life, let us not forget her after death."
S. AMBROSE.

-- ---

" Innocens manibus et mundo corde."

LONDON: BURNS AND OATES.
1878.

Ballantyne Press
BALLANTYNE AND HANSON, EDINBURGH
CHANDOS STREET, LONDON

TO the many and dear friends of Dora, who have begged me to furnish them with an account of her last illness, I offer these pages, together with the prayer that they will of their charity say a " Hail, Mary" for her and for her adopted Mother.

AIGLE, 1878.

PASSING AWAY.

NEW YEAR'S DAY.—What a lovely warm
day it was, the air balmy as in summer,
the sun bright, flowers blooming in sheltered
places in the fields, the rose hedges showing
buds and leaves, the sun unclouded. It seemed
a day full of bright promise, and I, too, was full
of hope for my Dora.

When I came from church in the morning she
was much amused at my account of the people
I had met, women and children all carrying
large parcels and hurrying along with happy
faces. "Le jour de l'an" is the great day of all
the year here in Switzerland, as it also is in
France; families meeting together—friends and
relatives exchanging presents.

In the afternoon our doctor's wife and daugh-
ters came to see us, bringing with them a goodly

basket of "gateaux" as a New Year's "cadeau."
Dora was in great spirits, showing them all the
presents we had received from home, and offering them her little gifts. She looked so animated, so well just then, that it was hard to
realise the delicate state in which she really was.
But still her cough clung to her, and every day
she seemed to become a little weaker. For the
first time she began to have her breakfast in
bed, and though I endeavoured by every means
in my power to tempt her to eat, it was very
seldom I succeeded. She tried one thing after
another, but tea, milk, coffee, and chocolate—
all seemed, after a while, to disagree with her.
Frequently, after having taken food, she rejected
it ; still when she got up about ten o'clock she
was always busy—had no difficulty about dressing herself or doing her hair, and never asked
or seemed to want any help. She was, as she
had ever been, bright and lively, and always
ready to enter into any little project which was
on foot. For instance, I had bought a fox skin,
and wished to have it properly tanned. We had
the address given us of a person at Lausanne

who was a very good furrier, and she proposed
to write and ask him his price before sending
him the skin. "One must always be on one's
guard in dealing with these people," she said.
"You had better not write yourself, Auntie dear,
you cannot write sufficiently like a man; let me
do it, and I will only sign my name D. T——."
She was greatly delighted when the answer came
addressed to M. T——, and flattered herself
that the reasonable price the furrier had asked
was entirely due to his having imagined her to
be a Swiss, and of the male sex. "He would
have asked four times the sum if he had guessed
who we were," she remarked; and indeed I
believe he would.

In addition to her other occupations, she
would often employ herself in concocting little
dishes for dinner, having all the materials
brought into her room. She liked very much
to make curries, a dish in which she especially
excelled; and, with the aid of an Etna, she
managed all her little cookeries wonderfully
well. Then she would generally spend an hour
or two every day in drawing, of which she was

very fond, and I always encouraged and excited
her to persevere in it. Had I, however, known
the state in which she was, I should not have
insisted, as I often did, on her employing herself in household matters. But alas ! I had no
conception then of the weariness it must have
caused her to attend to her accounts and direct
the servants. She never made any complaint,
never objected to performing any of her accustomed duties, only sometimes she would ask me
to speak to the " bonne" when any fault was to
be found. How often have I since reproached
myself that I did not fully appreciate her nervousness and weakness, and that I did not
prevent her from taking so much to heart the
doings of our cook, a rough, unpolished speci-
men of a Swiss domestic, whom she strongly
suspected of keeping her own family out of our
store of provisions. One circumstance which
occurred at this time I may mention here, as it
places in beautiful evidence a striking trait of
her character. She was about to engage a
servant, who had been highly recommended to
us, when our landlady came into the room to

warn us against her. In order to give us a reason for not taking her, Madame G. began to tell us of some very dubious passages in Marie's previous life. She was so voluble that I could not stop her; but very soon after she commenced her story Dora rose with her cheeks aflame and quitted the room. "Oh, Auntie," she said to me afterwards, "I cannot tell you how miserable it made me when Madame began to talk in that way of Marie. I never knew anything at all about such things until I read 'The Home of the Lost Child,' which Mrs. —— lent me, and I cannot bear to hear about them." She spoke with unusual energy and earnestness, her cheeks were crimson, and her eyes brimming with tears. "My darling, I wish I could prevent you from ever hearing anything of the kind," I replied, "but as long as you hate it and shrink from it you will get no harm. Look upon it as a trial, and offer it up to God and all will be well." She sobbed and was greatly distressed, but I began to talk of something else, and after a while she became cheerful and placid. It had always been the same with her, purity of heart and purity of speech had ever been amongst the most prominent of her virtues, and with perfect truth it might be said of her that she had never soiled the whiteness of her baptismal robe, whilst at the same time she was perfectly free from all prudishness and false delicacy. In this and in many other respects she bore a near and beautiful resemblance to that sweet Saint Agnes, whom she had chosen to be her beloved Patroness, and whom she loved with such a deep, unwavering, and personal affection.

For a long time past, Dora had not cared to take out-door exercise, she was soon tired and her clothes seemed too heavy a weight for her to carry. Still she persevered in going out for half an hour twice a day, but she shrank from doing more than walking up and down the path which led us past her doctor's garden, which adjoined ours. She was greatly delighted one day when he came to the gate, and seeing her admiring his roses, gathered a couple and gave them to her, at the same time promising her a bouquet of laurustinus as soon as it should be fully out.

It was a strange winter : if it had not been that the trees were leafless, one might have fancied that spring had really come. Every day I used to bring Dora a fresh bouquet of field flowers, oxlips, cowslips, primroses, and violets. Some I took up by the roots and planted in a basin, and she used to laugh and be very sceptical about their growing, but she was delighted when they threw out flowers and provided us with two or three improvised *jardinières* for our salon. She had always been fond of flowers and arranged them with the same exquisite taste which she showed in everything with which she had to do. One lovely day when we were out together, I well remember, the air was as soft as in June, the sky was cloudless, roses were blooming in the hedges which bordered the gardens. She had been silent for a long time; then she said, " Oh, Auntie ! is it not strange that this weather should seem made for me, and yet that I do not get any stronger ?" But whilst she was so weak her spirits were as cheerful as ever, although she became more and more nervous, and, whenever any of our friends came to see us

she would shrink timidly behind my chair and
flush painfully if she were addressed. As had
ever been the case, she was happiest in the
society of children, and always greatly enjoyed
having little Marguerite B. for her companion in
her afternoon walk. Her cough, which had now
lasted more than two months, and was attended
with great expectoration, diminished a little towards the middle of January, but the fever
which had so long been wasting her still continued with its alternations of heat and shiver-
ings ; yet she slept well, hardly stirring from the
time she went to bed until she awoke in the
morning at half-past five. At that hour she
always had a fit of coughing, but when it was
over she would fall asleep again and not wake
till I brought her her breakfast.

It was about this time I had a letter from a
dear friend at Florence, in which she said : " I
dreamed of you last night, and to-day, although
I feel very unwell, I must write you a few lines
because I want so much to hear from you. I
have thought a great deal about you lately, wondering what would be your plans for the New

Year. I hope it is not too late to wish it may
be a very happy one for you, and also for Dora.
You seemed in my dream to be so really here
in Florence, that I wish I might take it for a sign
you are really to come. I thought we were all
four walking together chatting away as though
we had never been separated. I did not feel as
if any of us were ill, or that any one of us
dreamed of being an invalid—yet for myself I
am very ill, the weather is damp, and I am
suffering a good deal with my chest. I hope
Dora is better. M. looks quite well, but, poor
child, she dreads leaving Italy. Oh, how weary
is life, how sad and unsatisfactory ! It seems to
me, with our blessed Faith, I, of all others,
ought to be quite weaned from everything here
below ; and yet I long for a little tranquillity—
some rest before I take the *last* journey of all.
Do you too not feel that you must be settled
somewhere ? I should love to have my home
here, but that cannot be. What will my poor little
child do in A——, where all our friends and
relations are Protestants ? I feel for her more
than for myself. But God will care for her ;

she is a dear lovely soul. We must pray much
for each other, I think. M. and I often talk of
you and Dora, and we long to see you both. I
hope we shall have this happiness ere long.
Could not Dora write to M. ?"

Dora had always been very fond of M.
She looked up to her as a real child saint, and
often sighed as she said how little she resembled
her. Any news that came from Florence was
ever welcome, and on the receipt of the letter
from which I have quoted a few passages, Dora
eagerly began to build castles in the air founded
upon our friend's wishes.

" I know it would not be possible for us to go
to Florence," she said ; " Dr. B. would never
hear of it ; but we shall be going to England this
year, and might not Mrs. N. and M. come to
us there on their way to A——? That would
be delightful, wouldn't it ?"

" Yes, indeed it would," I replied, "and
we will write and propose it."

Little foreseeing what the future had in store,
I joined her all the more heartily in trusting our
little scheme might be carried out, because

we were just then hoping that all manner of good things would result from a sojourn which our doctor intended Dora should make at Leysin, a village on the Alps, when the season should be a little farther advanced. She had already been there on two former occasions, and had derived immense benefit from the pure air which she had breathed at an elevation of all but five thousand feet above the sea. And we were all of us confident that equally happy results would accrue to her from a residence there on this occasion also.

It was, I think, on the 16th January, the same day on which we had received the letter from Florence which had given Dora so much pleasure, that she had also one from our good Curé, to whom a little before she had written to tell him of the permission we had received from the Holy Father to have Mass said for us in our own house, wherever we might be, and to say that we intended immediately to arrange an altar for that purpose. She added that we wished he would come and say Mass as soon and as often as possible, and she spoke of the deep happiness she and I felt in having so precious a privilege granted to us, and to her especially who had been so long deprived of it. Her eyes danced and her face was lit up with smiles as she read aloud his answer :—

"TRÉS HONORÉE MADEMOISELLE DORA,—

"Je partage de grand cœur la satisfaction que votre bonne Tante et vous éprouvez de l'insigne et rare faveur dont le Grand Pie IX. vient de vous gratifier. Croyez S. V. P. que j'en suis aussi, heureux que vous, et permettez-moi de vous en féliciter.

"Il faut que vous soyez en grande estime auprès de Sa Sainteté pour qu'il vous gâte ainsi : et je vous en fais mes complimens. Je vais être très fier d'être votre Aumônier, à commencer dès demain : J'irai dresser l'autel dès les dix heures afin que tout soit prêt pour jeudi, à l'heure que vous m'indiquerez.

"Aujourd'hui je suis obligé de partir tout à l'heure pour Vevey.

"Veuillez agréer, Mademoiselle, et faire agréer

à Madame votre vénére Tante, mes respects religieusement devoués,

"Votre Serviteur,

"A. Ch. B. Des."

Dora's joy was all the greater on receiving the good news as she had been afraid we should have to wait for the permision of the Bishop of Sion before we could have Mass said ; and when a box arrived from the Curé's with all the furniture for the altar, vestments, &c., her delight was unbounded, and she was very eager to have an oratory at once made ready. She was also most anxious to go to Confession and Holy Communion, but I told her that to assist at Mass would at first be excitement enough, although as soon as ever it was prudent nothing would make me happier than that she should enjoy the most precious of all privileges.

Thursday came : a fire was lighted in the great stove and the altar was decorated with flowers. At eight o'clock the Curé arrived, and never shall I forget Dora's look of ecstatic joy and thankfulness as we knelt side by side in front of the altar. She would have remained on her knees the whole time if I had allowed her, but after a time I made her sit down. Her cheeks were glowing, and she seemed wholly unconscious of everything but the celebration at which she was assisting. Ah! how lovely she looked in her grey dress and her long white veil; she seemed hardly to belong to earth, but rather to have already joined the angels. How little did I then dream that this would be the last time she would ever kneel by my side!

Her spirits still continued good; she felt sure she was making progress, and looked forward to the time when she would be able to take sketches at Leysin, and carry them away to England, to serve as pleasant remembrances of all the beautiful scenes she loved so well. Spite, however, of her thinking herself better, her doctor, on examining her, found that the left lung was in a very delicate state, though not as yet affected.

On the 29th of January the fever from which she had so long been suffering being still as high as ever, it was decided that she should remain in bed until it was somewhat subdued. Just before that time, Dora, still full of hope that we should be able to go to England this year, asked me whether she might not write to a relative of hers who had great experience of climate, and whom she thought would be sure to know of some place that would suit us both. When his answer came she was much pleased to find he had suggested Malvern, where the scenery was beautiful, and where, although there were no Swiss Alps, we should at any rate have English mountains. Even now that she had taken to her bed, we neither of us felt very anxious ; on the contrary, that she should be there was to me rather a relief than otherwise. Safe in her own room, I knew she would not be exposed to the currents of air in the corridor whither I had not always been able to keep her from going when she wished to amuse herself with her magpie, whose cage was there. Her bed was not as comfortable as it ought to have been, but as usual she uttered no complaint. I made her occupy mine during the day, but always thoughtful for me, she would creep back to her own early in the afternoon, spite of my remon-

strances, for fear mine should not be sufficiently
aired for the night. Even after she took to her
bed she continued to occupy herself with the
management of the household, and our daily
expenditure; but when I saw the effort it
cost her I told her I must henceforth see to
these things myself, and with a sigh, half of
relief and half of regret, she relinquished into
my hands the duties which had formerly given
her so much pleasure.

After Dora had been a week in bed, and had
not seemed to be gaining any ground, her doctor
told us that he wished we should go to Leysin
as soon as we could arrange to do so. The
weather was mild, and on the mountains it was
so warm, he said, that the peasants were working
in their shirt-sleeves. He hoped everything
from the effect of the mountain air, especially
as Dora had derived so much benefit from it
the previous year, when to all appearance she
had been almost as ill as she was now. Both
she and I were startled at first at the idea, but
we soon became reconciled to it. Dora was so
so sure Leysin would do her good, added to

which, if we went there now, she observed, we should be able to return to England in June instead of waiting till September, as we should have been obliged to do if we had not gone to the mountains until later on. For her doctor had insisted upon her spending at least five months there, in order that her chest might be strengthened as much as possible before we went home.

We had already engaged the Châlet Faure for a later period of the season; but now that it had been decided we were to go there immediately, I wrote to the owners, who were living at Lausanne, to ask whether it could be made ready to receive us at once. The answer came in the affirmative. Madame and M. would go up the next day to Leysin and have everything prepared, and on their way back they would call to see us. Three days afterwards M. and Madame made their appearance, and told us that the couple of days they had spent on the mountain had been charming. The sky was cloudless, the air soft, the sun so hot that excepting in the morning and evening they had not required a fire. They had driven down the mountain in a sledge; there was a good deal of snow, but not nearly so much as usual : all the peasants agreed that the "gros de l'hiver" was over, that there would be no more bad weather. The châlet was so cosy they were quite loth to leave it. We should be even more delighted with the winter view to be had from it than we had been with it in summer and autumn. Then they described the interior of the châlet—how well furnished was the little salon, with its sofa and easy-chair, and large table and library of books, its pictures and lamps. The bedroom which communicated with it must be appropriated, they said, to Dora and me, as it had a large stove in it, together with a wardrobe and wash-hand stand. They dilated also upon the charms of the little gallery running in front of the châlet, how pleasant and sunny it was, and what a glorious prospect it commanded of the Dent du Midi and the Glacier du Trient, whilst from the gallery on the other side of the house there was a lovely view of the Chamossaire and Diablerêts mountains. The kitchen, moreover,

was everything we could wish, fitted up as it was
with a potager and provided with all kinds of
utensils. Dora, lying in bed in the adjoining
room, heard all that was said, and when Madame
F. and her husband had left she called me to
her. Her eyes were sparkling, her face beam-
ing. "See, Auntie, what S. Joseph has done for
us ! it is a palace we are going to," she exclaimed ; "we have fallen on our feet at last, and
come into our fortune ! and I heard Madame F.
say she knows of a servant too, is it not delightful ?" Yes ! we were both of us thankful for
that, as it would have been very difficult to meet
with any one belonging to the plain who would
have been willing to go up to the mountains in
winter, and it would have been impossible to
trust ourselves to the tending of peasant girls
such as those at whose hands we had already
during the preceding summer suffered so much.
And then my child was so thankful to be rid of
the woman who had hitherto been with us, and
who seemed not to have a grain of kindly feeling in her character. All Dora's fears were at
an end; she was longing now for the day to

come when we might set off. She had not a
doubt as to the result, she was sure she would
get well. "Everything was for the best," she
said. "A little while before, and she would
much rather have waited until later on before
going to Leysin. Now everything was arranging
itself beautifully, and nothing would prevent us
from setting off for England in June." And as I
looked at my child's happy face, I felt as if my
heart were warmed by its sunshine, and I were
infected with her own bright hopes for the
future.

It was only just before her doctor had
ordered her to stay in bed that she had given
up writing to her young friends, and to the one
amongst them all whose letters she especially
valued. At the beginning of February she had
a letter from her, written under the impression
that we had already gone to Leysin, and recalling to Dora's remembrance an expedition they
had made last summer; also adding how fervently she hoped that ere many months had
passed away we should be coming back to Aigle
en route for England. Sad indeed it has been

to me to read that letter now, with its inquiries about the peasants—the facteur and his aunt, and all that Dora was to say to them; its congratulations upon our taking up our piano to the châlet, and its comments on the astonishment it would excite among the villagers!

Another letter which Dora received about this time, and which gave her exceeding pleasure, was from Rev. Mother of the Convent where she had once spent six of the happiest months she had ever known. Her face brightened as she read it, and told me how all at the Convent hoped they would be able to welcome us there some time during the coming summer. The house, Rev. Mother told her, had lately been enlarged, but not in such a way as to prevent it looking as it used to do. "Oh, how I long to see them all! What happiness it will be to go there and give them a surprise," she said. "We will not tell them anything about it, Auntie, and I will slip into the class-room just as I used to do and sit down in my usual place! And how delightful it will be to have a good slice of that delicious Convent bread and butter, such as

one gets nowhere else. And then I will go to
Sister Stanislaus and beg her to give me some
of her favourite pear jam, which you thought so
good, Auntie. Oh, it will be Paradise to go
there !" And then came a flood of happy recollection such as always used to burst forth whenever we had "a good talk," as she called it,
about her beloved St. M.'s.

On the 6th February, E. W., a young friend
of mine, arrived from England. Dora had been
looking forward with but little pleasure to her
visit, for she was always apprehensive as to how
she would get on with young people of her own
age, never feeling so much at her ease with them
as she did in the society of those very much
older than herself, or with quite young children.
However, E. had not been more than a few
hours with us before Dora was delighted that
she had come. I never remember her being in
better spirits, or laughing more heartily than she
did that evening over E.'s amusing anecdotes of
one of her brothers who had been a great friend
of my child's in earlier days.

All that week she was making various little

plans in connexion with the life we were about
to lead at the châlet, arranging for the daily
supply of food, &c. She never seemed to mind
being left alone whilst E. and I were out, and
yet she did not now care to read anything excepting her beloved prayer-books, which with
her rosary were always under her pillow. These
and her own bright thoughts were sufficient to
keep her happy and occupied. Often, too, when
we were not in the room, she would lie quietly,
sleeping or dozing at intervals. She still took a
lively interest in everything that had formerly
given her pleasure, discussed the "façon" of E.'s
dresses, and took great pleasure in showing her
the contents of her jewel case, out of which she
selected a few little ornaments to take with her
to Leysin. She was also greatly occupied with
settling which room at the châlet was to be set
apart as an oratory. For we hoped that at least
every fortnight we should have Mass said there,
and that she would be able to assist at it.
During the fortnight she had passed in bed she
had been able to hear Mass, which the Curé had
frequently said in the *salle-à-manger*, from her

own room. She had also once received Holy
Communion, but it had exhausted her so much
that I dared not accede to her wish to receive it
once more before she went to the mountains.
It had always been the deepest of her sorrows
and trials that she had been so seldom able to
go to Mass or Confession and Holy Communion, or to fast ; but, as in everything else, she
was resigned and sweet, and good and reasonable, though she could not conceal the effort it
cost her to submit to a privation greater by far
than any other she had to endure.

On Saturday, the 10th February, our doctor
finding the fever would not give way to any
of the remedies he had employed, decided we
should go to Leysin the following Monday. I
was much startled and alarmed, for just then
Dora seemed to me quite unable to bear so
fatiguing a journey; but after hearing her doctor's
reasons for the step he had resolved to take, I
felt there was no other course to pursue. My
child, on her part, appeared to be quite content not to wait any longer, though at first she was
a good deal agitated at the prospect before her.

It was settled that on the next day a man should be sent to the mountains to see in what state the road was, and whether it was practicable for a four-wheeled carriage, and if not he was to arrange that the carriage should be put upon a sledge at Sepey, a village at the foot of the Leysin mountain. Dora was also to get up and be dressed on the Sunday, that the transition might not be so great as it would have been had she been taken on Monday direct to the carriage from her bed. Although I had all along been looking forward to our going, yet now that the time was fixed I felt almost stunned. It was well I had no leisure to think, otherwise I am sure my courage would have failed me, and I should have utterly broken down. Even as it was I dared not look up to the snowy heights rising high in the air above us whither we were about to betake ourselves, and where we should be far away from all human help, from our doctor, and from the kind friends who had shown so much solicitude about us during my darling's illness.

There was much to be done during the few

hours that remained to me in the way of packing
and arranging what things were to be taken with
us and what to be left behind, and in straining
my memory to the uttermost that I might not
forget the many little matters which would be
needed for my child. I had also immediately
to telegraph to Lausanne to the servant Madame
F. had engaged, and desire her to come to Aigle
at once.

On the Sunday, after Dora had had her dinner,
she got up, and we made a couch for her with
easy-chairs and pillows in the drawing-room,
there being no comfortable sofa in the room on
which she could be placed. She was much
tired with dressing, and looking sadly pale and
thin, but I attributed a good deal of her changed
appearance to her having her hair down, which
always altered her greatly, and which whilst it
gave her the look of a child of some twelve
years of age, made her appear far more delicate
than she did when it was differently arranged.
In the course of the afternoon our landlady and
her daughter came to see her. Dora was very
unwilling to receive them, but gave way when I

said they would be very much pained if she left without having said good-bye. Madame looked serious and sad, and Dora said afterwards how much better she liked her manner than her daughter's, who, in order to cheer her, was gay and talkative, but who, as Dora remarked, did not seem to know how to treat a sick person. They told me afterwards that they were both of them much shocked to see her, and that they felt they had looked upon her for the last time. But I, recalling to mind how ill she had been when she had gone to Leysin the year before, and how rapid and surprising had been the change which the mountain air had effected, would not allow myself to believe but that she would derive equal benefit from it now.

In the course of the evening the guide we had sent to the mountains in the morning returned. The road, he said, was in a very good state; the snow, generally speaking, hard and beaten. There would be no need for us to take a sledge, excepting for the luggage. If Mademoiselle E. went also on the sledge the carriage, with five horses, would easily convey

Dora and me. The snow round the châlet was about four feet deep, but a path had been cut through it, and there would be no difficulty in reaching the entrance. Two men would go with us to clear away the snow when necessary. He was very cheerful about it all and very encouraging in his manner, but all the while my heart was sinking within me, and I felt as though the undertaking were a thousand times more formidable than it had seemed to me at first. Still, when later on our doctor came to give us his last directions, and to tell us what to do on our arrival, and how to manage everything for the journey so as to enable my darling to make it with the least possible fatigue, I felt my courage rise once more, together with the sure conviction that should all human help fail us God would Himself be with us in our hour of need.

The servant we had engaged arrived that same Sunday. Alas ! I had no sooner looked at her than I felt as though inefficiency were written on every feature of her face. Slight in form, delicate, and melancholy-looking, she was the last person I should have chosen for the position she would have to fill. But it was too late to make any change; all I could do was to hope for the best, only I had a sad foreboding that she would add to, rather than diminish, the burden I was already finding heavy enough to bear. Thank God, my darling did not know how heavy it was. I shall always be thankful for, always glad at heart that she but seldom saw me looking otherwise than cheerful, and that it was seldom, too, I allowed the expression of anything that was not hopeful and encouraging to pass my lips. If it had been otherwise, how different all would have been! Her faith in me, and her reliance on my word, was so entire and undoubting, I sometimes felt as if she thought I had the power of life and death in my hands, and that it was on me she depended for every breath she drew. Our doctor also—how implicit was the trust she had in him! His visits revived and cheered her as nothing else could do, and infused new life into her when all other remedies seemed to fail. This last evening of her stay at Aigle she was full of animation when talking

with him of all she would do when she got
better, and of the walk she would then take
through the forest to the Roc de Veyge, whence
she could look immediately down into his
garden, some three thousand feet below.   It
was arranged between them that the day before
she went on the expedition she would write to
him and tell him at what hour she would be
there, when she would put up a red flag, whilst
he was to do the same in token that he saw her
signal.   Then he was to come into the garden,
and she would look at him through her field-
glass.   My darling ! how little did she anticipate
that that very day fortnight she would be passing
away from all that she loved on earth, and that
it would be from Paradise she would gaze on
the spot she was looking forward to revisiting
with so much pleasure !

In former days, and especially during the last
summer she had spent at Leysin, her doctor had
been most kind in writing to her ; very proud
she was of his letters and very dearly did she
prize them ; and now when he promised to let
her hear from him very often, and told her she

must write to him in return as frequently as she could, it was most touching to see the expression of happiness and gratitude which lighted up her face. But though she felt that she had many compensations to make up for going to the mountains so early in the year, and at a time when she was so weak and ill, her chief source of comfort lay in the thought ever present to her mind, that she would thereby be able to go to England at the very beginning of summer. " You are sure that I may go there in five months ; you will promise me that I may," she said over and over again to her doctor and to me. I do not know whether in the secret of her heart she ever had any foreboding that she might not get better, but as she never concealed even the faintest passing shadow of a thought from me, I do not believe that a doubt or fear as to her ultimate recovery ever crossed her mind.

We were to set off at nine the next morning, so as to reach Leysin before it became too late in the afternoon. Dora slept well, but she was much tired with dressing, although she brightened

up when her doctor came with kind words of
encouragement and a little gentle scolding because she had been too "journey proud," as she
said, to eat any breakfast.

The carriage did not make its appearance till
long after the appointed time, and the delay
made my darling very nervous, though she bore
it with her usual sweet patience. I too was
anxious, and when, after sending one messenger
after another, there was still no appearance of it,
I felt almost inclined to countermand it, being
fearful that setting off so late we should not
reach Leysin before sunset. At last, about ten
o'clock, it arrived, and as the day was beautiful
and warm as summer, I thought it best to start.
A couch was arranged in the carriage with the
aid of cushions and camp-stools, and as soon as
all was ready the driver went upstairs to carry
my child down. But she would not hear of it.
"She could walk quite well," she said, and so
indeed she did with the help of our landlady's
arm; she even wanted to get into the carriage
without assistance, but this I would not allow.
Our hostess looked very serious when bidding

us good-bye, and as soon as we had started, and my darling had somewhat recovered her breath, she turned to me with a sad smile and said, " It seems as if Madame G. thought me very ill, she looked so exceedingly grave." " And so indeed you are, my poor child," I replied, " but we are going where, please God, you will quickly regain all you have lost during the last few months." She smiled, but made no answer. As we gradually ascended the Sepey road the heat continually increased, and Dora could not bear the weight of the shawls, wrappings, &c., with which I had covered her. I too was obliged to put off my jacket, bonnet, &c., and would have had the windows open if it had been safe for Dora. She lay quietly on her improvised couch, looking very pale, but perfectly calm and cheerful. Every now and then I persuaded her to take a little bit of biscuit and a spoonful of weak brandy and water, for I was afraid lest her strength might not hold out through the long and wearying journey we had before us.

It was not till we got to what is called the Halfway House that we met with any snow.

First we saw it lying in a partially half-melted state on the sides of the road, then gradually becoming more solid and thicker, till at last there was only a track wide enough for the carriage to pass slowly along. The pastures all around us—the sides of the mountains—were entirely covered with a white glistening mantle, whilst beneath the same spotless covering ·the dark roofs of the châlets were also hidden. It was a strange, weird, beautiful scene, and the utter calm and silence which prevailed, unbroken by song of bird or lowing of oxen, contrasted sorrowfully with the anxious turmoil of my own spirits. At one o'clock we reached Sepey. What a different aspect the village wore from that in which we had hitherto been wont to see it in the lovely summer or glorious autumn seasons, when everything around seemed to breathe of joy and exultation! Now it was all so sadly desolate and *triste*, spite of the bright sunlight, that it made one's heart fail to think of any of one's fellow-creatures passing their days in the midst of such solitudes, and surrounded by such dread, cold, unsympathising mountains.

I had already written to the landlady of the hotel at Sepey, and desired her to have a fire lighted, a bed made ready for Dora, and dinner prepared. On our arrival, my child was carried at once to her room. She was greatly exhausted, and I made her drink some wine, which revived her a good deal; but spite of all my persuasions, it was only a very little food that she was able to swallow. During the hour we rested, the luggage was taken off the carriage, and a sledge arranged for E. Again Dora was determined to walk downstairs; but this time she did not object to being lifted into the carriage, and once more we set off. The exertion had rendered her painfully breathless. As soon as she was a little better she turned to me and said, with a smile I shall never, never forget, "Oh, Auntie, it is so difficult to breathe;" but not one word of complaint, not one sign of fretful irritation, did she show. "And you are so patient, my darling," I replied. "I am sure if I were in your place, I should be very different." "Oh no, no, no," she answered, "I am not patient; you do not really think so, do you?" "Indeed

I do, and I am sure you have been patient always." She said nothing, but shook her head, smiling the while, and then closed her eyes, only opening them from time to time to look at the progress we were making, and to welcome with pleased recognition the familiar peaks of the Tour d'Ay and the Tour de Mayen, as they gradually disclosed themselves to view. It was very difficult to believe they could ever look different from what they were doing now—the snow which covered them seemed so solid and so everlasting ; the fir-trees, too, were so black and motionless, one could hardly realise that spring would ever have power to infuse into them renewed life and bright colour.

We had not ascended far before some men, who were working near one of the châlets, prophesied that we should find it impossible to reach Leysin with the carriage ; the driver, however, only laughed, and replied that there would be no difficulty. If there were not difficulty, there was certainly discomfort enough to encounter, as every now and then our vehicle lurched heavily in places where the snow had

drifted and the road was narrow. At other
times we had to halt whilst our pioneers cut
away the snow ; and sometimes we were obliged
to leave the road entirely, and plunge through
the snow-covered fields. When we got to the
Crête, the highest part of the ascent, a bitter
wind suddenly blew from the other side of the
pass, and although the windows were well closed,
it was not easy to prevent it from penetrating
into the carriage. But my child assured me she
did not feel it; and after a few minutes, when
we had crossed the ridge, we felt it no more.
It was here that we first came in sight of
the Glacier du Trient. "Oh, how glorious—
how glorious it is !" Dora exclaimed ; "it is
worth while coming here in winter only to see
that;" and indeed, in other and happier circumstances, I should have said the same. It
seemed like the revelation of another world,
brighter and more lovely by far than any of
which our every-day experience could give the
least idea. Ethereal in its beauty, angel-like in
its white purity, every peak, every slope was lit
up by the radiance of the sun, as they rose into

the fathomless blue, cloudless sky above. Ah,
how indescribably lovely it all was, and yet how
indescribably sad !

At last we came in sight of the village, and
very thankful I was that we were drawing safely
to the end of our anxious journey. The snow
was four feet deep round the châlet, and although
a path had been cut through it, even I was
obliged to be carried into the house. The
stove in our bedroom had been kept lighted
for some days, so that the room was comfortably
warm ; and, as soon as possible, I undressed my
darling and laid her in bed. She was greatly
tired and exhausted, but still she did not seem
to lose heart ; and after she had rested a while,
she entered with interest into all the little
arrangements which I told her we should have
to make before we could feel settled. There was
a large bed and a small low iron couch in our
room. She wanted very much to occupy the
couch, which was placed in front of the windows, so that I might have the comfort of the
large bed ; and when I would not hear of it,
she said, in the sweet tone which was so peculiar

to her, and the decided manner I knew so well, "Very well then, but, Auntie, remember it is only for to-night." At nine o'clock I gave her her medicine, and she slept tolerably, though once or twice she woke to cough, but after the fit was over she soon fell asleep again.

The next day (Tuesday, 13th) the weather entirely changed, a violent wind had risen in the night, and from morning to evening we had nothing but showers of sleet. It was a dismal prospect out of doors, and within there was but little to cheer one. We afterwards heard that in the valley of the Rhone the weather had been still worse; the mountain stream between Ollon and Bex, about three miles from Aigle, having overflowed its banks and committed dreadful ravages, ploughing up the high road and covering it with *débris.* It was better then after all, I thought, that we were at Leysin, and that we had made our journey thither the day before; for we could not have managed it had we delayed it, as I had at first thought of doing, for another twenty-four hours.

But I was disappointed that my child had no

appetite, and that there was no diminution in the fever. Yet it was too early, I said to myself, to begin to be disheartened; the change and fatigue and excitement of the day before would be sure to tell their tale upon my dear one's feeble frame; I must try to be patient and hopeful. Then there were household annoyances to contend with —our servant proving as utterly inefficient as I had feared she would. She knew nothing about the making of soups or any dishes suitable for an invalid; the beef-tea she prepared for Dora was like dish-water; she was stupid and dirty; I felt at my wits' end. It was impossible I could keep her; all I could do was to write at once to Aigle, and beg one of my friends there to try and get some one in her place. My darling was sadly concerned and wanted still to direct household matters, as she had been accustomed to do; but this I would not consent to, though I was sometimes obliged to go to her for directions respecting little matters on which I painfully felt my ignorance. I had been so accustomed to leave everything to her in times past, that now I was quite bewildered at having to take them in hand myself. There were also many other disagreeables from which I would have saved her if I could, but it was impossible. Her bed was placed against the wooden partition separating us from the kitchen, and through it the slightest noise was heard. Whenever a pan was taken down or replaced, the clanging noise would startle and distress her, though she bore it all most sweetly and patiently, sometimes laughing at herself for having become so nervous.

I would gladly have removed her into another room, but there was no other which could be heated. Though our châlet was quite the best in the village—a palace compared with the others—it was constructed on the usual plan. The entrance was from the side gallery, and the ground-floor was divided into three rooms— kitchen, bedroom, and sitting-room—all communicating with one another, the bedroom being in the centre and containing a stove which was said to heat the sitting-room also, though it did not do so in the least. Above were four bedrooms, in none of which was there a stove, whilst not one of them was large enough for Dora and me.

Our first day was spent in arranging our stores and unpacking our boxes. The bulk of our luggage—the piano, &c.—was to have been sent up that day, but the weather being bad it could not be despatched from Aigle.

On Wednesday Dora was to have got up, but she was too tired, added to which the weather still continued stormy. Heavy clouds hid all the more distant Alps from view, and through the mist which shrouded the nearer heights we could only dimly discern the dark forms of the Chamossaire, the Diableréts, and the Chaussée mountains. Magpies were constantly flying round the house, their discordant voices and the hoarse croak of ravens being the only sounds which, together with a loud rushing wind, broke the silence. My darling was less feverish that day than she had been at Aigle, but she coughed a good deal. As ever, she was gay and cheerful, often laughing heartily at my little domestic perplexities. The visit of the "facteur" was the only event f our day. He always arrived about half-past

one, and was our *one* link with the civilised
world. To him we entrusted all our commis-
sions, and on him we had solely to depend for
our supplies of bread and meat, and in fact for
all our food; for there was not a shop of any
kind in the village, not even an inn where we
might have procured necessaries in time of need.
He also brought our letters, and every day went
with a message or a note to our doctor. Oh!
how eagerly I used to open his letters; it was
as though he alone, on earth, could save my
beloved child. How eager, too, was my child to
hear what he had written; how anxious to try
every fresh remedy which he suggested; how
desirous to comply with his reiterated wish that
she should take more nourishment!

Thursday was a lovely day; the sun shone
brilliantly; my child seemed better, and my
spirits rose. After breakfast I went out for a
little walk on the gallery. A peasant was
passing. I asked him what he thought of the
weather. " The winter is past," he replied, " we
shall have no more snow, it is melting quickly."
And so indeed it was. Already I could see

shrubs peeping through it; here and there it had melted from the châlet roofs and was falling from the fir-trees; the brook which ran down the lane was no longer altogether hidden, and although the fields around us were still one unbroken expanse of snow, I thought it was not possible for it much longer to resist the heat of such a sun as was shining in the heavens. The air was so warm and genial that I was obliged to exchange my winter jacket for a shawl—my heart was full of hope. "Surely Dora must get better now," I said to myself. "Oh! how thankful I am we came here."

In the afternoon E. and I dressed her, and she came into the sitting-room, walking without any assistance. She lay down on the sofa, and amused herself with remarking upon and suggesting various changes in the position of the furniture; but she soon became tired, and before teatime I proposed that she should return to bed again.

The sun was just setting, and I threw the shutters back that she might see from her bed how glorious the Dent du Midi looked clad in its rosy mantle. She gazed at it in silence for some time, with a smile on her lips and that ethereal heavenly expression in her eyes which I have never seen in any one else, and which others besides myself have often remarked. Then I exclaimed—" Dora, it seems so strange! we are actually ourselves in the Alpine glow; the snow all round us is as rosy as it is on the Dent. It is so beautiful. I wish you could see it." Alas! she never beheld it on earth! That night she was very ill, the fever was higher than ever. Once she answered me in an abrupt, nervous voice, which frightened me greatly, and made me feel at once that she was not herself. I gave her a composing draught, which calmed her, but still her cough distressed her a good deal, though after a while she fell asleep. Towards morning she looked so pale and wan that I was terribly alarmed. At six o'clock I sent for a peasant girl who had been accustomed to do little errands for us, and telling her Mademoiselle Dora was very ill, begged her to go at once, and if possible by the short path down the mountain, and take a note from me to the doctor, in which I entreated him to come up to us as soon as he could. Very anxious were the hours which followed, until about twelve o'clock Aline returned with an answer from our doctor. He wrote to say that he had that moment received my letter, and would set off for Leysin at once, for he could not and would not leave me any longer a prey to the anxiety in which I evidently was. In my fear and bewilderment I had begged him to let me take Dora back to Aigle; any risk seemed preferable to remaining at Leysin, so far away from him. But he said that to take such a step would be to renounce all hope of saving her, especially as she was suffering from rheumatism, which would be increased by the damp air of the plain.

It was well I did not know, whilst awaiting our doctor's arrival, that a portion of the road between Aigle and Sepey had been carried away a couple of days before by an avalanche, or I should have quite despaired of his being able to come to us. As it was, he was obliged to leave his carriage and horses on one side of the breach and cross on some planks which had been laid down to the other side, whence he went to Sepey on foot, and there hired a sledge to convey him the remainder of the way. He had set off quite early in the morning, but the journey, at all times a long one on account of the continual ascent, was rendered still more tedious by the breaking down of the road, consequently it was about three o'clock before he arrived, " bringing," as my child said, " hope and cheerfulness with him." But the cheerfulness and the hope were in his words and manner only, not in his heart. I am sure that from that time he had given up all hope of saving my beloved child, and I felt, though not till some time afterwards, that in the few words he spoke to me when we were alone together he had been trying to prepare me for my coming sorrow.

Dora's whole face lighted up when she saw him enter the room, though at first she said but little, only lying quietly on her bed and smiling as she looked at him ; after a while she told him she had felt very thirsty all day, but was afraid of taking lemonade, of which she was very fond, lest it might disagree with her; great then was

her pleasure when he made her a glass himself
and told her to drink it whilst he was there, and
he would guarantee that it should do her no
harm. Alas! he knew that there was nothing
now that would do her either good or harm.
Then he asked her whether there was not anything at all which she could fancy, and whatever it might be he would get it and send it to
her. But she only shook her head and told him
she had everything she wanted. The preserved
beef which had been sent to us from England
she seemed to relish more than anything else,
but beef-tea and oatmeal gruel formed her
favourite sustenance.

After her beloved doctor had taken leave of
her and she had said her adieux with a yearning,
wistful, loving expression in her eyes which, he
afterwards told me, he should never forget, I
went with him into the gallery, and asked him
what he thought of her. He looked very grave,
and said that everything depended upon our
being able to subdue the fever. But shall we
succeed?—he paused and shook his head. He
had hoped the mountain air would have

diminished it at once, as it had done in such a wonderful manner on former occasions, but instead of that it was higher than ever. He dared not give her any stronger medicines than those she was now taking, and he did not see how she could battle with such fever much longer. Her system had indeed, in a certain sense, become habituated to it, still a time must come when it would give way. But while there was life there was hope, and we must still go on using the remedies which we had been trying during the last month. Then he spoke of getting a *garde-malade* to share in the night watching. I too was anxious to have some help, for I was afraid of my own health giving way under the continued pressure of anxiety and fatigue. All day long I was on my feet, and for the last six weeks I had never had anything but broken rest, whilst of late I had been constantly up during the night with my poor child. Our doctor added that he would try and send a Sister of Charity—he preferred them to any nurses, and he was sure both Dora and I would like them better—at any rate, he would lose no time in

E

sending some one. And then he left me with a heart weighed down by care, and feeling it a greater effort than ever to appear cheerful when I went back to my child.

She did not, according to her wont, ask me what her doctor had said, but I told her of his wishing to send some one to help me. At first she seemed distressed, and then blamed herself, saying she was sure I must be sadly tired, but would I not always sleep in her room? I assured her I would, and then she was quite satisfied and even pleased when I said that most likely a Sister of Charity would come to us.

After I had been with her a while I went out to breathe a little fresh air on the gallery. My heart was very full, and I could not help shedding tears as I paced up and down, praying to God to give me strength to bear whatever might be in store, even should it be the sharpest of all the trials I had ever known, and He should call upon me to give up my darling into His hands. All around was so lovely and so peaceful, I felt as if the calm of Heaven were about me, and yet as though I could hardly feel its soothing influence, the strain upon me was so great. The solitude and silence too oppressed me, we seemed so far from all human help—from all sympathy of friends and relations. It was a hard, hard trial to be so completely alone, and if it had not been that strength was given me from on high I know not how I could have borne it.

I fancy the excitement of her doctor's visit had been too much for my child, great as the pleasure it had given her had been at the time ; she had a disturbed night, and the fever rose as high as forty degrees. She was also very sick and retched violently, whilst at one time she was evidently wandering in her mind. I was up all night with her, and at five o'clock in the morning wrote to our doctor telling him of the state she was in. But, as always, I had to wait eight or nine hours before getting a reply, and what a wretched, anxious time those hours of waiting used to be ! At last the facteur returned, and handed me a note with directions as to what I was to do to stop the sickness and retching which exhausted my poor child so sadly.

I was also to give her a soothing medicine for
her cough, which had been more than ordinarily
troublesome, and I was not to be afraid of
administering cognac if she appeared exhausted,
and if her skin were tolerably cool. He also
said that our good Curé had written to one
of the chanoines of S. Maurice begging him to
obtain a Sister of Charity for us ; he therefore
hoped Dora would soon have "une bonne sœur
grise" sitting by her bedside.   In conclusion, he
begged me, in his kindness, to write the next
day, and indeed every day until I could send
him the good news that she was better.

Although on the Thursday and Friday nights
Dora had been very ill, she seemed better again
on Saturday.   She was constantly dozing, owing
partly to her being so weak and partly to the
soothing medicine she was taking.   But Dr. B.
said I must not allow myself to be anxious on
that account.

I think it was on that same Saturday I began
to read prayers to her, as she told me she could
not collect her thoughts sufficiently to say them
herself.   The night before she had complained

of feeling very sleepy—she did not think she could pray.

"Well," my darling, "I will pray in your stead, and I am sure God will hear me," I replied; and that seemed to comfort her.

Saturday afternoon was fine, and she was bright and cheerful, interested in the letters which came, as well as amused at a mistake made by a young friend of hers in addressing a newspaper to me as Monsieur B. "Tell her, Auntie, when you write, that I said she must have been thinking of *im*"—alluding to some little joke which had passed between them.

That day, too, she got up to have her bed made, and was entertained at all the precautions I took in wrapping her up, saying that "indeed she did not require so much care to be taken of her." She arose and returned to bed without assistance, and indeed up to that time I did not perceive much failure of muscular power. But, alas! all the strength she had was derived from fever, and she maintained it to the last. After she went to bed she exclaimed—

."What a long time I am, Auntie, in taking a turn !"

"Well, dear," I replied, "we must have patience, and be as hopeful as we can."

She had asked some days before whether we might not have a Novena made for her to our Lady of Lourdes, and whether she might not take the Lourdes water. I had gladly assented, and told her we would begin it in a few days, which would give me time to write to as many friends as possible and ask them to join us in it. She was much cheered by the prospect, and seemed quite sure our Blessed Lady would work the same miracle in her behalf which she had done four years ago. At that time, being very ill, I had taken her up to London to consult one of the most eminent physicians there respecting her case. After examining her lungs most carefully, he told me there was no hope whatever of saving her, and that he did not think it possible her life could be prolonged more than, at the outside, three or four months, so far was she gone in consumption of the worst kind. A fortnight afterwards he told me that her right lung was

completely honeycombed with tubercles all running into one another; she had become almost
a skeleton, and was wasting quickly away.

It was then that it was suggested to us by the
Confessor of the Convent where we were staying,
that we should make a Novena to our Lady of
Lourdes, and ask as many religious as possible
to join in it. I did so, and we began the
Novena. A few days afterwards I took Dora to
our doctor. He was examining her with the
stethoscope, when he suddenly turned round to
me, and with an expression of surprise on his
face exclaimed—

"Why, Mrs. B., the child is better!"

"Do you think so?" I asked.

"Yes, I am sure of it," he replied. "Go on
as you have been doing, give her plenty of milk
and the tonic I have prescribed, and bring her
to me in a fortnight's time."

When I took her again to his house he again
examined her with the stethoscope; and again
he turned to me with even a greater expression
of surprise on his face than he had exhibited on
the former occasion.

"What have you been doing to the child, Mrs. B. ?" he cried out; "she is cured, the tubercles have healed."

I thought it was then time to tell him that we had been making a Novena to our Blessed Lady of Lourdes. He listened to me in silence. Strict Protestant as he was, I could not, of course, expect him to believe that Dora's cure was owing to the Novena, but I was very much gratified and touched when he observed that he could assure me it was not owing to any skill on his part or to any remedies he had employed—for indeed he had used none excepting the administration of a simple tonic—that Dora's cure was owing. Then turning to her, he told her she must be very thankful to God who had restored her, when no human means could have been of any avail, and affectionately warning her to be very careful and prudent in future and not to spend the ensuing winter in England, he bade us good-bye.

From that time my child's health continued to improve, though she was always fragile and delicate. The sojourn we made on the Alps in

the year 1874 did her immense good, and if
it had not been for an attack of rheumatic fever
which she had at Montreux, in 1875, she would
have passed a very good spring. As it was, she
gained so much health and strength when we
were at Leysin during that summer, that we over-
persuaded our doctor to allow us to return to
England, and it was immediately after our
arrival there that all the bad symptoms from
which she had suffered two years previously
began to appear once more. There seemed
nothing for it but to return to Switzerland as
early in the spring as was practicable. But,
alas ! it was too late—the evil had become too
deeply seated ever again to be remedied.

But my child evidently believed she had been
in a far worse state on the occasion of our
making the first Novena than she was at present, and therefore she was most hopeful as to
the result which would follow from making
another now.

Having received answers from most of the
friends to whom I had written, we began our
Novena on Sunday morning. All that day she

was so weak and nervous that I was miserably
anxious, and to add to my wretchedness, the
facteur told me when he made his appearance
late in the afternoon that he had forgotten the
letter I had asked him to take to our doctor.

In the afternoon the piano and luggage, which
could not be sent up earlier owing to the breaking down of the road, arrived, and the new
servant also came. Dora was a good deal distressed by the confusion that ensued.

" How strange it is that I am so nervous," she
remarked. " They will not come into our room
with the boxes, will they? And I need not see
the servant, need I ?"

I assured her that no one should come
near her, and that in a few moments all the
bustle would be over; then I kissed her
and soothed her as well as I could till the
nervous agitation passed away, and her face
resumed its usual tranquil happy expression.
Louise, the servant we had engaged, was no
stranger to us. Dora knew her well, and liked
the idea of having her. I too had hoped she
would prove a great help and would be able to

prepare little dishes which Dora would fancy. But, alas! that very evening I found she was as inefficient almost as the one we had sent away, and I saw that until the nurse arrived—and, as yet, none could be found—we must go on as we had been doing. Everything seemed to turn against us, and if it had not been that from morning to night, and through the night also, I was obliged to be up and doing, and therefore had hardly time to think, I should have been ready to despair. Spite of all, however, I felt I had cause for thankfulness that matters were not even worse. E. was with us, and she was a great comfort, though I was anxious about her also, for she was not strong, and I was fearful of overtaxing her strength and her nerves, unduly strained as they already had been by all that she and I were going through. But in her loving-kindness she had begged so earnestly I would take some rest, that at last I consented to go to her room for the first portion of the night, though it was not to sleep, for I lay awake, listening for the slightest sound, till I could bear it no longer, and going downstairs I took my

usual place on the little bed in Dora's room.
How I bore so many sleepless nights, I know
not. But God was very merciful, and enabled
me to keep up till the end came.

Sunday night my child slept calmly, and all
through Monday she seemed much better, saying, " She felt sure it was owing to the Novena."
I too began to hope again, for she looked so
like her old self. After dinner, when she heard
me ordering more beef, she said with a smile,
" Why, Auntie dear, are you ordering beef again ?
You will be ruined if you go on in that way.
It is high time I should be up and taking the
housekeeping in hand again."

I confessed that indeed I did feel very
ignorant, that I knew nothing about these
things, and longed that my little housekeeper
could resume her duties. She looked at me
very fondly and said, " Poor Auntie, it is sad
I can do nothing for you ! What a trouble
I am."

Then the letters came, and among them
was one from an old friend of ours answering
a note which Dora had written to him in

January, and the reading of which seemed to give her great pleasure, bringing back as it did to her remembrance many memories of the happy time we had spent at Whitby some years ago, several incidents of which she took delight in bringing back to my recollection. She was also much pleased with some ornamented note-paper that had been sent to her from England, sitting up in bed examining and arranging it. That same afternoon our kind friend, Madame Drapel came to see us. She had always been very kind and much interested in Dora. The previous summer we used to have long talks together sitting in front of her grange, and I had always looked upon her as quite my beau-idéal of a Swiss peasant. She asked for Dora, and was much distressed when I said she was too ill to see her. But I took her into one of our little upstairs rooms, and very touching it was to hear her relating all the little incidents in our last year's intercourse which had struck her in " Mademoiselle Dora," and made her look upon her as a little saint on earth. Her affectionate words and her deep piety consoled and en-

couraged me very much, and when she opened
her basket which she had brought with her, and
told me it was full of "merveilles," a cake which
she knew Dora was very fond of, and which
Madame was famed for making, her eyes filled
with tears and she could hardly speak, as she
tried to say, that perhaps "Mademoiselle Dora
might fancy them when she could not eat anything else." After she had gone I went into
Dora's room. She had heard Madame Drapel's
voice, and could not imagine what we had been
talking about. I told her Madame had been
speaking of her and had brought her a basket
of her favourite "merveilles." She asked to
see them and tried to eat one, but it was in vain ;
she had lost her taste for them, and put them
aside saying she was afraid they would not agree
with her, asking me at the same time to give
them away.

It was strange that every day when our former
bonne had made my bed she would persist in
putting a railway rug, which I was using instead
of a blanket, with the black instead of the
scarlet side outwards. Dora remarked that it

looked very dismal, and I took care to turn it.
Our new servant did exactly the same thing, and
though I knew it was foolish, the sight of it, I
am ashamed to say, made me always uncomfort-
able, it looked so exactly like a pall spread over
the couch. The improvement which had appa-
rently taken place in my dear child lasted until
Tuesday evening, though her appetite had at
that time entirely failed her. Our doctor was,
as usual, very wishful she should take some
nourishment, and in his daily letters mentioned
several things which he thought she might fancy.
Some meat lozenges, which are made at a
French convent, were the only things, she said,
that she cared to have, and they were accord-
ingly ordered for her. Tuesday night she
was very ill again, her cough distressed her
greatly and the fever ran higher than ever. I .
wanted to bathe her face and hands with eau de
Cologne; at first she refused, fearing it might
make her cough, but afterwards she found it a
great comfort. It almost broke my heart to behold her sufferings; whilst it was beautiful to
see her bearing them with such sweet patience.

My anxiety was very great, all our efforts had seemed to be in vain, and I did not like to see her during the day so constantly dozing; but Dr. B. again assured me that it was only weakness made her do so, and I must not on any account attempt to rouse her, for that whilst she was asleep she did not cough. All this he said in the letter he wrote to me on Wednesday, in answer to the one I had written describing her state on Tuesday night. But with it came another letter to be delivered to me privately; in it he said he was more grieved than he could express at the sad news I had sent him, and that it was not possible to augur anything good from the state of the dear child. It was almost impossible, too, that she could much longer battle with such an amount of fever as she was undergoing. We must, however, try once more to subdue it, in the hope of succeeding—but should we succeed? Alas! it was not likely. Then, he added, " Believe me that it was not without suffering real anguish of heart that I urged you to go to Leysin, as a last resource." When I read this paragraph I did indeed feel

as if my anchor of hope had given way, and I
was drifting on to the dark gloomy sea, with
no earthly light to guide me—oh, the anguish of
that moment! And yet even then I was asking
myself whether something of my darling's increased illness ought not to be attributed to the
weather. Heavy snow was falling, and she had
always been sensitive to every change. But
whilst I said so, I felt at the same time as it
hope had died within me. When I went in to
Dora; she was looking better, and E. was
combing out her long hair, whilst she was re-
gretting its coming off in the way it had done for
so long. Then she washed her face and hands
herself, and looking up at me with a smile said,
" Did you ever see such hands, Auntie dear?
they are just like birds' claws." I could not return
her smile, nor did I dare to speak; my eyes
were full of tears which, dear child, she happily
did not see, for she went on speaking of various
little things which at last made me smile, and
enabled me in some degree to regain self-
control.

On that day I received a telegram from the

F

Curé, telling me to be of "good courage," for he was going to send me a young person in whom I might place the utmost confidence. It was not possible to obtain a Sister of Charity, but he was sure Marie would prove everything I could desire. He knew her well; she had attended a relation of his own during a long and serious illness—I must have no fears. I told Dora, and she seemed to be satisfied. All the afternoon she was constantly dozing, and it was with difficulty I persuaded her to eat a little, though she was quite willing to take from time to time some weak brandy and water. Wednesday night was not a very bad night, and she coughed less than usual. Thursday was lovely; I opened the shutters that my child might see the view, and the sight seemed to cheer her, though the light was too strong for her eyes. She was so quiet and cheerful that E. and I went out for a short walk along the solitary road leading to the forest, where my child and I had so often been together in the lovely summer time. Then the village used to be full of life; in the fields the peasants were working whilst

the children were playing in front of the châlets.
Now how changed everything was, silence and
solitude everywhere ! During the winter season
the men are employed within doors, carpentering,
and mending, and making additions to their
châlets, whilst the women are occupied in spin-
ning. The châlet doors were all closed to keep
out the cold ; no living creature was to be seen
as we passed along the village street ; once or
twice a cart laden with wood brought from the
forest passed us, but that was all. We could
not get very far along the road on account of
the snow being too deep, but we managed to
reach the cemetery, whence we looked down on
the valley of the Rhone surrounded by ranges
of snow-clad mountains. It was a warm, bright
sunny day, and very lovely was the view ; but
it was oppressive too, for not a sound broke
the silence—neither song of birds nor running
waters—it all seemed too still, too desolate, too
unearthly to belong to any other region than one
of which death had taken possession. Even the
brilliancy of the sunsets we had had since we
came to Leysin, seemed to have no spirit of life

within them, and the glorious starry nights gave
me no comfort as I gazed at the familiar con-
stellations which shone with such steely splendour upon the white world beneath them.

On our return to the châlet I found letters
awaiting me. One was from Dora's dear friend
E., saying how anxious she was to hear from her ;
how sure she felt that she would have written if
she had been well enough. Alas ! how little
she realised the state in which my darling was.
" You will write to her and tell her all about me,
will you not, Auntie ?" my child said ; but she
made no remark on E.'s saying she trusted the
pure air of Leysin would restore her to her old
self, and that she would ere long be as strong
as ever. There was also a letter from Fr. L.,
who was then giving a mission, saying he would
pray and offer up his mission work for his dear
child "Dotty," the pet name she used to bear,
and which, when she changed it for " Dora,"
she said she would like Fr. L., and Rev. Mother,
and one or two other friends, still to give her.
Her eyes filled when I gave her his message.
" We must trust in our Lord and His Blessed

Mother; say so to Dotty with my love, and tell
her not to forget me. I have always felt as if
she quite belonged to me. When she dies, she
will have a big crown for her innocence and
patience."

I had a letter also from my son, full of anxiety
about the state Dora had been in when I wrote
the preceding Friday, but trusting she had im-
proved, and that I had been able to take her
down to Aigle. How strange it seemed to read
those words, and then to look at my child lying
on her death-bed. Dora had rallied so wonderfully in times past, he went on to say, that he
could not despair even now. He trusted this
might prove a crisis in her illness through which
she would safely pass. "Give my best love
to dear Dora," he said; "tell her how we all
sympathise with her, and how much I trust that
God in His mercy will give her health again,
and that there may be many happy days in store
for her yet."

That afternoon, Marie, the young *garde-malade*,
arrived, and her appearance pleased me much;
she had a sweet, sensible, serious expression,

and spoke with a low, pleasant voice. But I saw my darling was very nervous when I told her she had come. I had, indeed, hardly ever seen her more distressed, though she made a great effort to overcome her emotion, and smiled when I assured her I would not leave her—she must not be afraid of that—I would still sleep in the room; the only difference would be that, knowing Marie was sitting up, I should be able to get a little sleep. Then when she was quite calm and reconciled to the idea, I called Marie in; for I knew that the longer the seeing her was put off, the more nervous my child would be. When Marie came to her bed-side, Dora smiled and spoke cheerfully, but when she sat down I saw that she did not much like her staying in the room, so I asked her not to remain there too long at first, until Mademoiselle Dora became accustomed to her. She sat up with us that night, I remaining on the little couch; and I was glad to see how gentle and nice she was in her manner with Dora, and how well she arranged her pillows, &c. By the morning Dora was much more reconciled to having her. "It is such a comfort that she is a Catholic, Auntie," she said. In a little while she asked me if I would not give Marie some work, and then she would not feel so nervous as she did when she was sitting by her doing nothing. She told me that there were some kitchen aprons to be made, and described how they were to be cut out with least waste of the material, just as she used to do when she had the charge of all household matters. And there was quite a pleased look in her eyes as she lay watching Marie plying her needle. She remarked also on the neatness of her dress, and wished we could have her for our servant always.

Hitherto my child had always worn her dressing-gown in bed, but on the Friday evening she asked me to let her put on her little scarlet flannel jacket, as the seams in the dressing-gown hurt her shoulders. It was very difficult to get it off, for the exertion affected her breathing painfully; but when she had changed it and her night-dress, she said she felt very comfortable; and now there was nothing to be done but to have her bed made. She got out of it herself, but remarked that her legs felt very strange; then she laughed, and said she might have been having champagne; but still she seemed wonderfully strong when sitting on the chair, and did not appear to be more fatigued than was to be expected when she got into bed again. It was not until that day that I saw how sadly she had fallen away since she had come up to Leysin. Her poor arms and legs were nothing but skin and bone; but there was hardly any change in her face, and it was that which had all along deceived me. During the last fortnight she had had frequent *mouches de Milan* applied to relieve the pain and palpitations she suffered from; but as she always liked to dress them herself, and to change the linen, I had hardly seen her chest until that day. It was a sad shock to me. I could hardly control myself whilst her bed was being made. As soon as she was laid again upon her pillows, and seemed inclined to sleep, I went out for a little while. I felt as if I could not remain in-doors, but must go and

walk for a while on the gallery, in order that I
might strive to regain composure. It was a
lovely day, though a little snow was constantly
falling. When I went out a number of magpies
flew away, flapping their wings and uttering
discordant cries. Ever since we had been at
Leysin, they were continually coming in flocks
to visit Dora's poor little magpie, whose cage
was in the gallery; and then they would fly off
and sit on the roofs of the châlets near our own,
chattering for hours. After a while, being afraid
that the noise of my footsteps would disturb
Dora, I went down into the village street. As
I was passing the châlet where we had lived two
years ago, I saw our former landlord, M. Tauxe,
and his wife, working in their grange. · They
accosted me, and asked for news of " Mademoiselle Dora." I could only shake my head,
and tell them I feared there was no hope.
" Helas !" M. Tauxe said, " l'année qu'elle etait
ici j'avais cru qu'elle avait gagnée sa cause."
Alas ! and so indeed had we all thought that her
wonderful recovery then was entire, and would
prove lasting. I could not talk with them, my

heart was too full. They looked serious, but it is not in the nature of mountaineers to show much sympathy; nor do they look upon death in the same light that we do. Life has but few pleasures for them—it is hard and rough and dreary; and when the end comes, they are, generally speaking, content to go and be at rest. Nor do they lament, as we do, the passing away of the young—they rather feel it is a blessing that they should be early taken away from the life of hardship which in all probability is in store for them. In all the village of Leysin there was, I believe, no one, with the exception of Madame Drapel, who could in the least sympathise with me, or who, after my child was taken, had a tear to give to her memory. This was one of the reasons which made me feel so utterly alone. I longed for some kind person of my own age to whom I could a little open my overcharged heart, and from whom I could receive help and comfort. All those about me were so young; our servants were gentle and kind, but quite inexperienced; and although E. was full of tenderness and sympathy, there was no elderly person at hand to whom, from time to time, I could appeal for counsel, or on whose experience I could rely in time of need.

On Friday afternoon my poor child had an attack of diarrhœa, which I knew was a very serious symptom, and I was much alarmed. The fever also was very high. When she tried the thermometer and found it was over 42°, I could hardly believe her, but alas! it was too true. I was sadly distressed, and again more than ever felt how terrible it was at such a time to be so far away from our doctor. The first part of the night she was very restless—alternately shivering and then complaining of her skin burning. One moment I had to cover her with additional shawls, and the next she would ask me to remove them. I bathed her face with eau de Cologne and her poor dry hands, and she thanked me with a smile. At last she fell asleep

It was a wild night, and the wind howled round about the châlet. About two o'clock in the morning I heard a noise in the gallery; a stifled cry; the passage of feet overhead; a window opened and shut. I guessed but truly the reason. A cat had jumped into the gallery where Dora's magpie was, and had pounced upon it. The " bonne," hearing the noise, got up and opened the window ; but it was too late, the poor little bird, which the cat had dropped on Louise making her appearance, died in her hands. I had hoped Dora had not heard anything ; but the first thing in the morning she asked me what had happened. I said the wind had been very high, and perhaps Louise had got up to see whether the windows were fast. She seemed satisfied with my explanation ; and I was very thankful that not then knowing what had taken place, I therefore had nò occasion to tell her of the suspicions which had sent a chill through my heart and compelled me to exclaim, " Absit omen." I was thankful, too, that there was no need to wound her tender heart and distress her with the sad tidings of the untimely end of the little bird of which she was so fond.

All Saturday heavy snow was falling, but during the morning Dora seemed better and had no return of diarrhœa. In the afternoon I

had a note from our doctor saying that he
greatly regretted he could not come up to
Leysin to see us at once, but he was ill with an
attack of rheumatism. As soon as he was able
to move he would be with us. As long as the
fever was so high I must administer larger doses
of quinine, returning to the smaller ones as soon
as it was a little subdued. He did not wish her
to take so much gruel whilst she was having
diarrhœa, but rather soup *à la farine*, such as
the peasants were accustomed to make.

The facteur also brought me a letter from our
dear Rev. Mother of St. M.'s, saying that the
sad account I had given of Dora had been a
great shock to her and to all the community,
although at the same time they felt it was wonderful she had lasted so long. They had begun
the Novena at once to our Lady of Lourdes. I
must be quite sure they would not fail to pray
for the recovery of one so dear to me. The
doctor who had attended Dora when she had
been ill at the Convent would be dreadfully
sorry, Rev. Mother said, to hear how ill she was
—he always remembered her with so much

affection. She asked me to give Dora their united love, and to tell her how earnestly they would all pray for her. If God willed to take her to His own Divine heart, Rev. Mother was sure she would not forget us. Though she knew well I was very sad about my dear child, still she could not help feeling it would be a blessing and a favour if our dear Lord took her to Himself before He took me, because no one would be left to care for her as I had done. After reading Rev. Mother's letter, I gave my darling the message she had sent; but I did not read the paragraph in which she spoke of her not getting better, for in her weak state I greatly feared to alarm her. "Dear Rev. Mother, how sweet and good she is; oh, how I should like to see them all at St. M.'s once more!" she exclaimed; and then she smiled and again said how she would like to have a slice of the delicious Convent bread and butter, it would do her so much good, she was sure. I do not know whether it was then or at an earlier period that something which was said led Dora and me to remark how differently nuns looked upon death from the way in which people in the world did. They never seemed afraid of it, but always dwelt upon the happiness beyond, and seemed to fancy it was quite natural to do so, and that everybody felt as they did. On looking back, I remember now that in the prayers I had always read to Dora and the passages I chose from the Bible—and especially from the Psalms—I quite unconsciously selected such as had reference to our passing away. "The Lord is my shepherd, I shall not want," was the one I felt sure comforted her most of all. It was the same with the prayers I used; but she never made any observation, although I am sure she followed every word, and especially the one which I repeated every day, and of which these are the words :—

"Oh, most amiable Jesus. I commend myself into Thy hands this day and for ever, as Thou, when dying on the Cross, didst commend Thyself into the hands of the Father, and as Thy most Blessed Mother commended herself to Thee. Make me to live according to Thy will and to die in Thee. And I pray Thee to grant the same to all, as well my enemies as my friends, through the merits of Thy Passion and Death, and through the intercession of Thy most sweet Mother and of all the saints. Bless me, O loving Jesus, with the Father and the Holy Spirit, and lead me to the life everlasting."

Knowing her love for our Blessed Lady, I daily added that beautiful prayer :—

"Oh, my Lady, Holy Mary, to thy blessed keeping and to the bosom of thy tender compassion I commend my soul and my body, this day, every day, and at the hour of my departure ; all my hopes, my consolations, my anxieties and miseries, my life and the end of my life, I commit to thy keeping, that by thy most holy intercession and merits, all my doings may be guided and disposed according to thy will and that of thy Son. Amen."

Then came the prayers for the Novena, with the responses, which she always said herself in a clear, distinct voice, never once omitting them up to the very last. And when our reading was over she would kiss me, and thank me and look calm and happy.

That afternoon, in addition to the other letters I received, was a note from Chanoine B., in which he said that when two days before he had sent me a note by Marie proposing to come to Leysin and give Holy Communion to Dora, he had intended to do so without letting her know that it was by way of Viaticum, as I had imagined he would, and which I was afraid would have alarmed her too much. His intention was simply that she should receive it by way of piety and devotion, and he still thought this was the best course to pursue. For until her doctor had entirely given her up, it would be wrong, he said, to occasion her undue emotion and excitement. He added, that he had asked one of the chanoines of St. Maurice to go to Aigle the following day to say the parish Mass, which would enable him to come up to Leysin, unless I sent him word that his visit had better be postponed. It was a great comfort to me, and to my child also, to feel that we were sure of having our kind Curé with us for the Sunday. She had so longed that we could have Mass; and when she felt how impossible it was that

G

she would be able to leave her bed and assist at
it in the little oratory I was intending to prepare
upstairs, I suggested that we should fit up an
altar in the salon where she could see it from
her bed, or we would arrange it in her own room.
How happy she was, and how she looked forward to the coming of the Curé, I shall never
forget.   She had been so afraid that it would be
impossible—and then it was such weather for
him to come up the mountain, she said.   But I
reminded her how little priests thought of such
things, and that I was sure he would not only feel
it a pleasure but a duty to do all he could for her.
I think it was on that sad Saturday, separated by
so few hours from the fast approaching sorrowful end—sorrowful to me, but oh! how sweet
and blessed for my darling—that I had a letter
from our dear friend at Florence, whom I had
asked, with her child, to join in the Novena.

"Very sad," she said, the sorrowful tidings
about Dora had made her, and very deeply
she sympathised with us both.   "Poor dear
child," she continued, "long and patiently she
has suffered and hoped.   But let us not lose all

hope yet. Our dear Lady of Lourdes came to her rescue once; she may do so this time also. Pray that, if it be the good will of God, Dora may still live to be a comfort and blessing to you who have been a true mother to her—so faithful, so loving and patient. I can imagine how dear she has become to you, and how hard it would be for you after all these years of waiting and watching to give her up. My dear friend, I pray God to avert this blow; nevertheless, we have His holy example before us, how, when sorrowful even unto death, He bowed meekly His will to that of the Divine Father. I read this most sorrowful and solemn history just after receiving your letter, and it seemed to me that in this inexpressible sorrow of the Sacred Heart of our dear Lord we might find strength for our greatest sorrows, peace such as He can give, and which He will always give without fail to all who come to Him, for has He not promised it? Come unto me *all*, and I will give you rest. Dear friend, if your child lives or if she dies it will be well with her—it will be well with you. Do not fear, it will be *best* for you both whatever

is His will. I often think of the great tenderness with which our Blessed Redeemer spoke to
His disciples that last day. How loving, how
inexpressibly thoughtful for their welfare; how
gently He persuaded them to trust in Him—to
believe in Him. 'I will not leave you comfort-
less,' He said; 'be not afraid, I will come to
you.' And oh! how true it is that He in His
abundant love always keeps this blessed promise
to all His own.

"I hope, dear friend, for the best. M. and I
will begin the Novena to our Lady of Lourdes
this evening. I think of you and Dora always;
and every day in my prayers, feeble and poor as
they may be—yet from an affection which is ever
reminding me of you—I mingle you and Dora's
hopes and fears and desires with mine, and so I
know does dear M. also."

On that evening, about seven o'clock, my
child had a fit of coughing attended with great
difficulty of breathing, although she had been
tolerably calm all day. I felt her whole body
and heart trembling; it was like a bird fluttering
to get loose; her face was set and pallid, but in

the worst of her distress she gasped, " Don't worry, Auntie, I shall soon be all right; don't cry, I am better now." Cold sweat stood on her forehead—she made me feel it and her nose, which was icy cold. She expectorated a great deal, and told me it was like strings in her throat. At the end of two hours the coughing ceased, and I gave her a *calmant* with some gruel. After taking it she slept quietly all night, not even waking or starting when the *cruche* fell on the floor and made a loud noise; so that I think she must have been unconscious, even though from time to time she moaned faintly, or coughed a little.

At five o'clock on Sunday morning I wrote to Doctor B. telling him how terribly ill my darling had been the previous evening; how great her sufferings were, and how much they had exhausted her, imploring him to come up to us at once. Even though I had then given up almost all hope, still I clung to the belief that whilst there was life all was not lost; at any rate, I thought he might alleviate her sufferings, and tell me what to do in case she had another "crise."

I also wrote to the Curé beseeching him to
set off for Leysin immediately, and not to lose
a moment, lest it might be too late; and I
begged him meanwhile to pray that both my
child and myself might be resigned to the adorable will of God, whatever that will might be.

On the Sunday morning when Dora awoke,
to my intense astonishment and exceeding
thankfulness she was quite bright and like
herself; her face had resumed its own cheerful, placid expression; her lips were red and
her eyes softly bright. Almost the first words
which passed her lips were to ask if the Novena
were over. I told her it would not be until the
following morning. Then she took the water of
Lourdes, and repeated the second clause of the
" Hail, Mary" quite distinctly, and in her usual
voice. I sat by her bedside nearly the whole
morning and read her a few prayers; after which
she lay quite quiet and composed, with her eyes
fixed earnestly upon my face. I shall never
forget the strange feeling which came over me
as she thus gazed. It was as though every
event which had taken place in her young life

from the time when she first came to me, a little child, passed before me. Most vivid, however, of all were the pictures which memory called up of our happy days in Rome, our visits to the different churches, our frequent drives in the Campagna, our daily occupations, down to the most trivial and insignificant amongst them all; her dresses, the hats she wore, the way in which her hair was arranged, her tones of voice, her voluble Italian, the snatches of songs into which she would suddenly break forth, and especially her favourite hymn to Mary Immaculate, which was seldom a day absent from her lips; her gaiety; the sweet, earnest expression which would come over her face whilst listening to Fr. Mulooly's eloquent descriptions of the underground church of St. Clemente, when taking her hand, he gave her the touching story of St. Alexis, or recounted the miracles worked by St. Clemente. All was present to me, not one link missing in the chain which bound the happy past with the sorrowful present; not one hour forgotten of all those in which year after year we had held sweet commune together.

At last I could bear it no longer; I could neither command the expression of my face nor the tone of my voice, so I went into the next room for a little while in order to try and recover the self-control I had so nearly lost. Even then my child looked so much like her own old self, so bright and well—lifting herself up in bed, and moving her pillows without seeming to suffer from the exertion—that I could not realise she was near her end. I thought the suffering of the previous night had perhaps been a decisive crisis, and that now she was going to get better. It would not, I said to myself, be a greater miracle than had been worked upon her formerly—I had seen her quite as ill, I fancied, the year before, and she had rallied and become strong again; why should she not do so now? I knew that Dr. B. feared the fever, but that also I began to hope might subside. So possessed, indeed, was I by the idea that the crisis was past and Dora would eventually recover, that I took up a book on climates to see whether there were any place mentioned which would be likely to suit her better than Aigle during the

ensuing winter. For, even if she recovered, I
knew we could not go to England; it would be
running too great a risk.

That morning she had had some gruel, and
at twelve some beef-tea and a veal cutlet, which
she ate with great relish. I went into her room
after she had had her dinner, and kissed her
and told her how glad I was, and she looked
pleased and happy. Soon after the Curé arrived.
He had received my note at seven o'clock and
had set off immediately, only halting at Sepey
till a sledge was made ready for him. I was very,
very thankful to see him, and when I told Dora
he was come she was not in the least agitated.
In a few moments he went into her room.
After talking for a little while she told him she
would like to make her confession that afternoon and to receive Holy Communion by way
of Viaticum the following morning. I had left
them alone together, and whilst I was in the next
room the facteur came to the door; beckoning
me out he gave me two letters, one made into a
packet, which he said the doctor wished me to
read privately. My heart turned cold within

me, for I felt that I knew but too well what
that message meant. In his first letter he said
he had sent me some soothing powders, to be
given to Dora morning and evening. He also
advised me to let her frequently breathe the
vapour of vinegar through a sponge. With the
exception of the soothing powders, I was to
give her no other remedy. "It makes me very
unhappy," he concluded, "to receive such bad
news as you sent me this morning, and it would
be a great comfort to learn that the dear child
has obtained some relief. I will go to Leysin
as soon as possible and see her."

In the letter marked "private" he told me it
was but too evident that our dear sufferer was
approaching the end of her troubles, and that all
which could now be done was to soothe and
calm her. "Since the moment in which I
found," he continued, "that Leysin had pro-
duced no diminution in the fever, as it had done
during previous sojourns there, I no longer
entertained any hopes. The oppression from
which the dear child suffers arises from the lung
which had hitherto been in a relatively healthy

state having been attacked at Aigle during the latter part of her sojourn there, and the oppression which she imagines is rheumatic has its origin solely in the lungs. I hardly dare venture to say to you, Madame, that my dear patient is in such a state that I should feel it to be a blessing if it were not to last much longer. Although I can absolutely do nothing for her, and my presence will be of no avail, I will come up to Leysin early to-morrow morning, and should the snow not allow me to go at that time, I will come as soon as possible afterwards. I will not add more to-day. Alas! I have, perhaps, already said too much."

Just as I had finished reading the letter, which was indeed the death-blow to all my hopes, the Curé came into the room. I gave it to him in silence—I could not speak. All I could do was to lift up my heart in prayer to God to sustain me during the hours that were before me, and to enable me to preserve calmness and composure so that I might not in those last dread moments distress or disturb my darling. Then feeling as though my prayer were already answered, and that strength was being given me from on high, I went to my child with a smile on my lips and anguish in my heart.

In the morning she had said that she thought part of her difficulty of breathing came from her heart, so I had advised her to put on a *mouche de Milan.* Fearing, after what the doctor had said, it would irritate and trouble her too much, I asked her to take it off, which she did. Then she said—" Why has Dr. B. left off the quinine ?" for I had told her she was not to have any more medicine.

I answered, " My darling, he fears the fever is too strong to be subdued, and he thinks the time is come for us to put our trust in God alone."

" Am I very, very ill then?" she asked.

" Yes, very, very ill ; but you know even now God might work a miracle in your favour, only we must pray to submit to His will, whatever it may be."

" Oh ! I do not want to die, "she cried, " and yet I would rather go before you, Auntie."

I told her it was hardest for me, for that God

was asking me to give up the joy of my life and the light of my eyes.

Then she said—" I should have liked to live and *soigner* you when you were old. Oh, Auntie, why have you loved me so much ?"

" My darling, you are not afraid of death, are you ?" I asked.

" No, but I am a little afraid of purgatory," she replied.

"But I am sure you will not be long there— not five minutes," I said.

" Are you sure I shall go to Heaven ?" she inquired.

" Yes, perfectly sure," I answered.

"And you will not be long in coming, will you, Auntie ?"

I told her I would not if God would let me, and that in the meantime she must pray for me, that I might be made ready to go to her.

She said she was afraid she might not be able to do *that.*

Then I asked her if she did not remember that we begged the saints to pray for us.

" Yes, but I am not a saint," she remarked.

" But you will be," I replied, " as soon as you
get to Heaven—because only saints can enter
there." And then I recalled to her recollection
what our beloved friend and confessor in Rome,
Mgr. K., had said about all three of us meeting some day in Heaven, and that we must make
a compact to do so; and she smiled at the remembrance. I reminded her also of what dear
Fr. L. had said about the large crown that she
would wear when she got to Paradise, and I
knew it would be a bigger one by far than
mine could ever be, because she had led an
innocent and holy life, and mine had been all
stained by sin.

" Oh ! do not say that, Auntie," she exclaimed.
Then she smiled and said—" But I do think I
shall get better. I have not *any* pain, and you
know our Lady of Lourdes worked a miracle for
me before when we had the Novena."

"Yes, my darling," I said, " I am sure she
will not refuse our petitions now, but she may
give us something different from what we expect, and something that will be far, far better
than what we have asked her for now."

She only answered with a smile. Then she spoke of the pain of dying, and how she dreaded the cold sweat coming and the agony. I told her that in the state she was in I did not think she would have any struggle; she would fall asleep, and pass away in her sleep into Paradise. I also spoke to her of our Lord, and asked if she could see the picture of Him hanging opposite her bed, and told her when she was suffering she would get great comfort and strength from thinking how infinitely more He had suffered for her sake. She said, " Oh, yes ;" and then she added, " I am so afraid I have not loved our dear Lord as I ought."

I told her all of us would have to say the same thing, even if we lived a thousand years.

" But I do not think I have ever willingly offended Him very much," she said afterwards.

When I reminded her of the love our Blessed Lady had borne her, and how she had been made her very own child, she took her medal of the children of Mary and kissed it fervently twice, once with a lovely smile on her face. I also spoke to her of the comparatively happy life she had always had, and how much trial and misery she would be saved if our Lord was about to take her now. She said, "Yes," but she would have liked to see them all at home in England. I told her I was quite sure she would when she was in Paradise. Then she asked if Dr. B. would not come again. She longed so much to see him.

I answered, "Yes, he was coming the first thing in the morning."

"Oh, I am so glad—so glad," she replied.

After that I left her for a time while the Curé went in and heard her confession. When he came to me afterwards he told me she had been perfectly collected, calm, and happy, and had still spoken of receiving Holy Communion the following morning. As soon as he had gone away from her she asked to see the *garde-malade* for a minute. She came to me after being with my darling, and I inquired what it was Mademoiselle Dora had wanted. She told me it was that she might ask her pardon "for having spoken," so she said, "impatiently to her in the morning :" but Marie could not remember it, and with perfect truth I can affirm that I never heard one irritable or impatient word pass her lips during her whole illness. She never complained of her sufferings, excepting when she had once said to me with a half-smile that went to my heart, " Oh, Auntie, it is so difficult for me to breathe."

She had no idea herself that she was so patient as she was, and I remember her laughing when a friend sent her a Christmas card at the end of 1876, and wrote on it " For my patient Dora."

" How little she knows me, Auntie," she said ; and she seemed quite incredulous when I assured her I thought she was very, very patient —far more so than I should have been in like circumstances.

The Curé, in common with us all, was astonished at her perfect calmness and serene cheerfulness. It was indeed a miracle worked for her by our Lady of Lourdes—the real answer to the Novena we had made to her—a priceless boon beyond our farthest reaching hopes; and it was all the more striking because during the last few weeks, although she had made every effort to overcome it, she had been painfully nervous, starting at the slightest sound, and saying that to hear any one speak in rather a loud tone made her heart beat violently. After the *garde-malade* had left I went back to her room. During the short time I had been away I had been preparing the chamber above for the Curé. The sound of moving about was too much for her, and she sent to ask me if it would soon be over; as I had just finished all that was necessary I went down stairs. As soon as she saw me she asked, "Auntie, are you sure the window is well fastened? for the Curé would be frightened if the magpie were to get in."

I said there was no fear; I was sure the window was fast. I hope she had no suspicion of the truth, and, indeed, I do not think she had, or she would have asked me plainly if her bird had been killed or if any accident had happened.

In a little while she spoke of being very glad she had made her confession.

"But I have been thinking since then," she

said, "that there is one sin I quite forgot to mention."

I inquired if it were anything of consequence. She answered, " Yes."

" Can you tell me what it is?" I asked; " and then I will speak to the Curé, if you like."

"Yes," she replied, "it is that I have had such a want of devotion; and that I did not feel glad enough when permission came from the Holy Father to have Mass said in the house." I then assured her that it was not a sin, that it would have been almost impossible for her to have felt sensible devotion, shut out as she had been for so long from all spiritual helps.

Of Fr. L., her especial friend, she always had been wont to speak with the most touching affection and gratitude for his loving-kindness and thought of·her. She had kept up an intimate correspondence with him ever since we had left England last year, and had only lately received a letter from him. Alluding to it, she said she would have so liked to see him once more. She wished he could have been

with her at the last.   But when I said, " Well,
my darling, you must try to think what a painful separation you have been spared ; and I do
believe it is in the great mercy of God that we
were brought here, where you are so quiet, and
nothing to disturb you."

She answered very brightly, " Oh, yes—yes !"

Then I said, " You will be cheerful and calm,
will you not, my darling, for my sake ?"

" Yes," she replied, and smiled and kissed
me.

" Now we must just submit ourselves in all
things to the will of our Lord, must we not ?"
She nodded and smiled again.

I next asked her if she would not send her
love to J. and to all her family at N.

" Yes, to J. and to all at N. ; and to E. and
to her baby, if it is born."

" You are quite happy now, are you not, my
darling ?" .

" Yes," she said, and smiled quite cheerfully.

Then I kissed her and said I was going
to get a little rest that night, and that please
God I would receive Holy Communion with

her next morning; and that as the Curé had only brought one host he would divide it between us, which seemed to please her very much. She had before told me that he had been "so nice and kind." At six she had a cup of gruel, and at half-past eight o'clock some beef-tea, which she said was very nice.

"It is what Mrs. W. sent, is it not?" she asked.

"Yes," I replied.

"It is the best of all I get," she remarked; "but I like Miss T.'s too. How kind every one at Aigle is to me!"

When speaking before of losing her, I had told her how sadly I should miss my little house-keeper, at which she smiled, and whispered, "Poor, poor Auntie," and stroked my cheek very fondly.

Then I went on to say I did not feel as if I were giving her up to go among strangers, but to be amongst dear friends.

"Think what you will feel when you see Saint Agnes, whom you have always loved so much; you must ask her to pray very hard for me;

and St. Joseph who has done so much for us both; and St. Clement too, and my own dear St. Peter. Oh! my darling, how I envy you."

She smiled very sweetly, and then I said, "You will see dear Mary G. too, and will you not be glad?" She answered "Yes," and added that she and Mary would be always near me, if they might.

When speaking of the fear she had of suffering the agony of death, I told her of my cousin Anne G., who just before her death had said to her mother—"Is this death? . Then it is sweet to die." And that seemed greatly to comfort her.

At nine o'clock she had her soothing powders, and then E. told her she would sit up with her, and Louise would also, in order that Marie might have a little rest as well as me. But she begged Marie might stay instead of Louise; and when I said she should, and asked her if she were quite happy now, she answered, "Yes, quite happy, Auntie dear," and kissed me and smiled. They were the last words my darling spoke to me—dear and precious words, which will be a comfort to me always.

For about two hours she slept quietly; then she awoke, coughing a little and looking so changed that E. asked her if she would like to have me called. She said "Yes," and in a few minutes I came down. When I entered the room I found it had already been prepared for the last sad and solemn office. The table near my darling's bed was covered with a white cloth, on which were the lighted candles and sacred vessels. My child was reclining on her pillows; her face was very pale and her eyes closed, but the peace of heaven was on her calm brow, and there was not a trace of suffering on her face. Her hands were folded, and she lay perfectly still. The Curé was standing near the head of the bed, whilst I took my place at the foot, and he then began the service. But just as he was about to give my darling Holy Communion, he exclaimed that he feared, as she had just then begun to breathe very shortly, she would not be able to communicate. She was unable to speak, but shook her head twice on hearing him say

this in sign she could swallow. Then he ad-
ministered Extreme Unction. In a little while
she said faintly, "Read some prayers in English." These were the last words my dear one
uttered. I read almost all the prayers for the
dying. Just as I reached the last clause she
made a motion with her hand for me to stop. I
do not know whether she did so because the
anguish in my voice distressed her, and that as
ever she wished to save me further pain, or
whether it was that her ears were no longer
conscious of any earthly sounds and were
already beginning to listen to the melodies of
heaven. After having paused a while, I kissed
her. She was quite unconscious then, and gave
no sign that she heard what the Curé said when
he whispered to her that she had the blessing of
the Holy Father with plenary absolution for the
hour of death. Nor did she seem to be aware
of it when shortly afterwards he gave her the
crucifix to kiss. Her face was still as placid as
ever, and still entirely free from all sign of
suffering. She was still reclining on her pillows,
with her hands on her lap, and she never moved,

excepting sometimes when she coughed a little
and expectorated, which she did without any
apparent difficulty. I could not bear to leave
her; but I found it so impossible to control my
grief—worn out as I was with watching and
anxiety—that the Curé took me into the room
which opened out of hers, and where I remained
until four o'clock, when I saw her once more
and kissed her. She had not moved, and still
her face was placid and peaceful, and like herself. I could hardly believe that she was unconscious, or that she was really dying. But
though E., who had been sitting with her all
through that sad night and who had her arm
under her head the whole time, had spoken to
her more than once, she never heard her; and
though once or twice she opened her eyes, it
was evident she saw nothing. The Curé went
to her very often, and gave her absolution two
or three times. He always said there was no
change in her position and no change in her
face. Every now and then E. gave her a tea-
spoonful of weak brandy and water. A little
after five she ceased to swallow, but there was

no struggle. She only breathed a little more faintly and a little more faintly, until at exactly seven o'clock in the morning she passed away.

On one of the lovely evenings which marked the last week of her life I had opened wide the shutters of the châlet windows, which were generally kept almost closed, lest her eyes should be dazzled by the brilliancy of the light reflected from the snows around, and lifted her up in bed that she might see the rosy sunset glow on the Dent du Midi, the mountain she had always so much loved. It was the last time that her eyes rested on anything outside her chamber. She gazed eagerly on the beautiful and familiar scene, while a bright smile played on her lips, and she exclaimed, "Oh, how beautiful! how glorious!" and then laid her head quietly back on her pillow. And it was at the very moment when the sun arose above the gleaming crest of her favourite mountain and was flooding its white slopes with light, whilst all beneath was in deepest shadow, that her pure spirit passed away to its home in heaven.

As soon as the last mournful duties had been

performed for her by loving and tender hands, and the treasures she prized above all others— her rosary, her Child-of-Mary medal, and the relics which until within the last few days she had always worn—had been taken from under the pillow where she had placed them, I went into her room. She had been removed from her bed to the couch I had been accustomed to occupy, and was lying there in her white dress, her feet lightly bound together with a piece of black ribbon, her fair hair gathered into plaits on either side of her sweet face, which looked even lovelier than I had ever seen it in life—the expression still the same, only deepened into entire peace and perfect happiness—her pale lips slightly parted, her eyes not quite closed; it was as though she were just about to wake from some placid, happy dream; her hands were clasped on her breast, and on them was laid a rosary, with which she had once touched the relics of St. Maurice and the Theban Martyrs. The little couch was placed close to the window, which was open; and the sun streaming in upon her seemed to transfigure her into an angel. I could not weep—my heart was full of thankfulness as I kissed her lips. In those first moments I thought only of her own exceeding gain, and nothing of my own supreme loss. Then the Curé and I knelt down beside her, and, together we repeated the *De Profundis* and the *Miserere.* After which, he read the prayers for the dead, and then I asked him to join with me in saying the *Te Deum.* It seemed almost the only thing that was meet for my darling. After we had ended it, I kissed her again, and left her for a time to the care of her young *gardemalade*, in whose hands I knew I could confidently trust all that was mortal of my dearest earthly treasure.

It was very, very hard to have to go away from the châlet and leave her there, but, alas! it was indispensable. The good Curé brought E. and me down to Sepey in a sledge. It was the first time I had ever been in one. How strange it seemed to me! The dazzling sun, the shining snows, the cloudless blue sky, the silence, everything on which my eyes rested, seemed so full at once of contrasts and harmonies !

At Sepey we rested for a while. The sad news had already preceded us, and we were received with kind sympathy by Madame A., who had known and loved my child. It was evening before we reached Aigle, but, instead of returning to my house there, we went to an hotel, for I felt that I could not bear to go back to the rooms which my child had once brightened with her presence, and which would henceforth know her no more.

Soon after my arrival a letter reached me from a beloved friend of many, many years, which comforted me greatly, and caused my eyes, which had been dry since my darling's death, once more to find relief in tears.

" My heart is very sad for you, in all your anxiety and dread for your poor darling," she said. " I think of you constantly, and wish you could be near me. But what good would that be?

"There is no help in such sorrow but one. He who alone can give you hope or comfort or resignation is as ever near you, His ear ever

open to your cry. He is not a God afar off.
If it must be that the child of so much care and
love is to be taken from you, you will give her
up in submission to His Will, sure that what He
wills is best. I am afraid that my words will
only pain you now, my poor friend, showing, as
they do too plainly, that I fear more than I
hope, but I cannot help writing as I feel. Life,
and young life, is still hers, and all may yet be
well. Give my dear love to Dotty. My poor
dear Dotty, how glad I am that she is so sweet
and gentle and patient! How beautiful will be
the memories she will leave you, my dearest
friend, and though to you the trial will be a
lasting and deep sorrow, how well for her to
leave the world ere she has been wounded by
human wrongs and sufferings, and to be with
her Saviour.

"Give her my tender love. To you too it
goes—faithful and true."

By the same post came also a letter from her
whom my darling loved to call her dear Auntie
M., and who had always loved my child with
especial affection.

"Poor Dora," she wrote, "and yet not to be pitied if she is so soon to gain her crown. Dear child, she, like Mary, has borne the cross of suffering and weakness without a murmur, through faith in our Blessed Lord. Accept, dearest, our prayers and sympathy for you both; for her, that her pain may be made easy by our dear Lord, and that if it be His Will she should not recover, that He will gently lead her through the dark valley of the shadow of death, and make it light by His mercy; for you, that whatever be His Will, He may be with you through it all, to comfort and support you. Ah! well I know He will, and that you will have strength granted to do and bear all that may be in store for you. I can think of nothing but Dora, and picture her to myself looking so thin and so patient that one can hardly wish to keep her here, but rather be inclined to envy her that she will so soon be in the rest of Paradise."

I was very thankful that in neither of these letters were there any wishes expressed for my darling's recovery; and most soothing to my heart were the loving words and tender sympathy which thus greeted me in my first sad hours of anguish and ere I could feel that the bitterness of death had passed away.

Another dear friend wrote: "It is only a near experience of death, and all other trouble of God's sending, that can ever rob it of its bitterness, and teach us to see and love our Father in sorrow as in joy. For dear little Dotty one can have no sorrow, save for the pain she suffers here; but my heart aches when I think of the void she will leave, *if* she goes, in her Auntie's fond heart.

"It is a comfort I cannot resist, to write the *if*, though any post may take it away, and I have little hope now; the doctor's notes have taken it all away, except in so far as whilst there is life there is hope—for the young, at least, if not for those advanced in life."

Early on Tuesday morning my darling was brought down the mountain in a hearse which had been sent from Aigle for her, the bonne and

Marie following in a *char;* the snow was firm and the descent was made without difficulty. As soon as the sad procession reached Aigle, the Curé and a cross-bearer preceding it, all that remained of my dear one was placed in the quiet little church, where she lay before the Blessed Sacrament all that day and night in her poor little coffin, made for her by one of the peasants at Leysin. And yet although it was poor and rude, I did not wish it had been otherwise. It looked more like the little bed in which I had so often seen her lying than the coffins to which we are accustomed in England, and which I can hardly ever look at without a shudder. Another painful detail to which we are obliged to submit in our own country is avoided here, where there is no hammering of nails to fasten down the coffin-lid, a hook-and-eye being all that is used ; as indeed it is all that is really necessary.

The next morning (Wednesday) her funeral took place. The day before almost every one I knew had sent me flowers for her ; and one dear friend had asked permission to decorate

I

the church with flowers and to "caress her with them," as she said, "in her coffin." In the evening, when I went to see her and the Curé removed the lid from her coffin, she seemed almost buried beneath sweet-scented violets and the loveliest flowers of spring. No change had taken place in her. She looked as sweet and placid as ever, and even her flesh had not the marble coldness which is so rarely absent from the dead. I could not realise I was looking on her for the last time, and that I had given her the last kiss until we should meet again, please God, never, never to be parted. My heart was quite full of peace—I felt that her soul was rejoicing in the presence of her God, whilst all that was mortal of her was resting in the presence of the Blessed Sacrament.

The next morning the sun was faintly shining through falling flakes of snow as we went to the church. When I entered I felt almost overpowered. It was decked with plants and flowers as if for a festival: the High Altar and the Altars of our Blessed Lady and St. Joseph were bright with lights and flowers; my darling's

coffin was almost hidden beneath wreaths of ever-
greens, white hyacinths, camellias, azaleas and
violets; whilst the crucifix at its foot was covered
with myrtle and orange blossom. It was a lovely
consoling scene, and one never to be forgotten.
The Prior of the Abbey of St. Maurice, with two
of the chanoines, said Mass. It comforted me
to think that it was to three such venerable old
men that had been entrusted the sacred office
of laying her to rest. The choir was composed
of boys who had also come from the Abbey
of St. Maurice, and very lovely both singing
and music were. At the close of the Mass the
Curé gave a touching address on the words
—ah! how applicable they were then beginning
to be—Rachel lamenting her children and refus-
ing to be comforted, because they were not.
Up to that time I had hardly felt conscious of
the prospect which was opening out before me,
when I should have to continue my pilgrimage
without my child by my side. But of these
things I cannot yet speak. There were very many
persons present. Every one who had known
and loved my Dora, and many who having only

heard of her were interested in her, had come
to pay to her the last tribute of affection, and to
me of sympathy.   After the sermon, and before
the sad procession left the church, several of the
ladies who had assisted at the Mass came up
and kissed me.   And then we took my child to
the quiet cemetery and laid her there, close to
the path along which she had been almost daily
accustomed in former days to pace, as being the
warmest and sunniest and most sheltered walk
we could find, and in sight of the mountain
which had ever seemed to her the realisation of
everything that is most lovely and glorious in
God's creation.

Ten days after her burial I went to her grave
—I had been too ill to visit it earlier, but the
hyacinths and azaleas were still as snowy white,
as pure and fresh and sweet as on the day
they had been placed there, although in the
interval the weather had been very stormy, and
both snow and rain had fallen.

Some weeks later a memorial stone was placed
at the head of my darling's last resting-place.
It bore the following inscription :—

IN

PACE ET IN CHRISTO.
DOROTHEA L. A. T——,
Ætatis xx.

In spe resurrectionis
Accessita ab angelis.
XXVI. FEB. MDCCCLXXVII.

Innocens manibus
et
Mundo corde.

"Amantissimæ et optime merenti fecit Nutrix pientissimæ."
A. M. R. B.

It was on the 26th of February, 1877, that
the Feast of the Sacred Crown of Thorns was
celebrated in Ireland, and very sweet it is to me
to remember that it was on that day my child
exchanged her crown of thorns for the crown of
glory which her dear Lord obtained for her by
the shedding of His most precious blood upon
the Cross.

*　　*　　*　　*　　*

For many years past it has been a custom at
the Convent of St. Clemente in Rome to draw,

on the Feast of the Epiphany, patron saints for the ensuing year, and Dora and I had always taken part in the lottery. In 1876 my saint had been S. Raphael, and this was what was printed on the card drawn for me :—

S. RAPHAEL, ARCHANGELUS.

24 *Octoberis.*

DILECTIO PROXIMI.

"Non te pigeat visitare infirmum, ex his enim in dilectione firmaberis."—*Eccl.* 7.

ORA PRO ÆGROTIS.

Surely it was not mere chance which had led me to continue praying for the sick for two months after the year 1876 had closed, and until the very day my child was taken. For by some oversight the cards from St. Clemente, containing our saints for 1877, did not arrive until the 26th of February, the date on which Dora passed away. When I looked at mine I was startled by its appropriateness. My patron saint, I found, was St. Joseph, and the inscription on the card was as follows :—

"MUNDITIA CORDIS.

"Ad hoc, sit totum studium tuum ut teipsam in pace et tranquillitate cordis possideas, et pro quocumque eventu non doleas, nisi de solo peccato.

"S. VINCENTIUS FERRERIUS."

The card which had fallen to my child's lot, and which came with mine, contained the name of St. Rose of Lima, and under it was this inscription :—

"HUMILITAS.

"Habent proprium mentes humilium, ut spiritualia dona habeant, sed in iis, quæ habent, se non attendant."

St. Rose of Lima! How many points of resemblance exist between her and my child? Of all the saints in the calendar, with the exception perhaps of her own beloved St. Agnes, there is no one, I think, to whom in her purity and innocence and fervour my child bore a nearer likeness.

Here it may perhaps seem as though my task might fitly end. And yet I think I should reproach myself afterwards if I did not add to my own story of the two closing months of my beloved child's life some few testimonies, taken from letters which I received after her death, of the opinion entertained of her, and of the love which was felt for her by dear friends who knew, and knowing, loved her.

One of the first letters which reached me was from Rev. Mother of St. M.'s.

"Since the receipt of the news of dear Dora's death," she says, "my feelings have been mingled ones of joy and sorrow—joy for the blessed soul which has gone to its happy home, and sorrow for you in the deep affliction which I know the separation cannot but cause you. I seem almost unable to pray for the dear child, but all day I am praying to her and asking her for favours which I know she will obtain, if she has any power with our Lord, as I am certain she has. With all my heart I feel that I can recite a Te Deum for her, and far better than I can a De Profundis.

"It is you, dear Mrs. B., who will need our prayers, and you shall have them too. I have already recommended dear Dora and you to the prayers of the community. As to the dear child herself, surely when she loved you so much on earth she will love you ever so much more in heaven ; and she will now have means of showing her gratitude by making intercession on your behalf. Let me again assure you that you shall have the prayers of us all for yourself, and the dear one who has been for so many years the object of all your care and affection."

Some few weeks afterwards, when writing to thank me for a mortuary card I had sent her, she says—"How applicable are the words 'Innocens manibus et puro corde,' inscribed upon it, to our dear child. She was, indeed, all the beautiful sentence expresses. I can with safety say that I never met with any one of sweeter or more amiable disposition ; her faith was something wonderful. She must have received from God a superabundance of that great gift. The Holy Father, the Church, and all its practices

were most dear to her, and she spoke on all such
topics with the greatest enthusiasm ; so much so,
indeed, that her young companions would listen
to her with rapt attention, and hang upon her
words. As the time drew near for her First
Communion her piety became intense, and in
approaching the altar for the first time she
looked more like an angel than a child of earth.
We were all struck by her appearance. She was
most cheerful in her intercourse with her companions, and enjoyed her little recreations as
heartily as any amongst them. She was also
most submissive to those in authority over her,
and the only fear she had was that of giving
pain or displeasure to any one. During the
tedious and trying illness which she had whilst
with us, her patience and cheerfulness never left
her, and she was most grateful for the least act
of care and kindness. This is not my personal
opinion only of the dear child, but is also that
of all who knew her during her too short stay
amongst us. . . . . Fr. G. L. was with us last
week. He and I had a long chat about your
Dora, and I found his impressions of the dear

child's virtue, sweetness, amiability, and piety very much the same as ours. The children of the Blessed Virgin's Sodality, to which dear Dora belonged, are going to have the beautiful photographs of her last resting-place framed for the little chapel where she so often loved to go and pray, as a memorial of her. I gave your message to L., who was very grateful for it. Did I ever tell you that, when Dora was leaving us, she gave L. a little picture and said, 'Now L., mind you *must* come,' meaning that she must become a Catholic, which, as you doubtless know, she did some time afterwards."

In another letter Rev. Mother, speaking of some violets I had sent her from my dear one's grave, says :—

" The odour was something delightful. We revived them in a little water, and placed them at our Lady's feet in the oratory of the Children of Mary, amongst whom Dora ranked on earth, and does so now even more especially in her eternal home. We shall certainly pray, as you wish, for the dear child, but we have continually prayed to her, and we do not invoke her in vain, for she-appears to delight in obtaining the little favours we ask. Over and over again I pray to our little angel when I am in any difficulty, and I remind her of her devotedness when on earth as an argument to urge her to persuade our Lady or St. Joseph to obtain for me what I want, and, like a good child, she always obeys my wish, if I may say so."

Fr. L., the dear friend to whom my child was so deeply attached, writes of her as follows :—

"When I first saw her," he says, "I was struck with the sweet innocence of the child ; she was bright and quick, and yet so perfectly gentle ; very sweetly simple, and yet with a tone of reflection more than one ordinarily sees in quite young people. She wrote delightful letters, so fresh and original ; no straining after saying clever things, and yet she did say clever things. As she grew older she was always inclining to better and higher aims in her own way of life, and in doing what good she could amongst those near her.

"The last time I saw her" (it was at St.

Leonard's), "she was suffering neuralgia, besides her general weakness. I noticed a little more of the woman in her then, but for all that she was still perfectly childlike. When you left the room I went to the sofa where she was lying, and said something to her about making good use of her sufferings and offering them up to God, together with the sufferings of our Lord. I cannot recollect precisely the words I used, but I know that very soon the tears were rolling down her cheeks. Whenever I think of her, I look upon it as a blessing to have been loved by so charming a child, and one who had always the fragrance of innocence about her. She must be following the Lamb now."

My dear friend at Florence wrote on the receipt of the sad tidings of my child's death : " Your little card tells a sad story, and from my heart I deeply sympathise with you in your sorrow. But for dear little Dora, ah ! how blessed, how beautiful for her this change which we call death, and which leaves such a void for us, but is the angel of life for her. You are right to ask us to say the Te Deum for her.

M. and I did so immediately after the De Profundis, and I felt, as the Curé of Ars said of a lovely young girl who died a most peaceful, angelic death, 'She is one of those souls that we need not pray *for?*' I feel that Dora has truly been purified through suffering, and therefore needs not our prayers, though from love of her we cannot choose but pray for her still. M. and I finished the Novena to our Lady of Lourdes the evening before we received the sad news of her death. M. said, 'Well, mamma, our Novena is finished, I wish we could hear from Dora now.' I replied, 'We shall hear soon, and I think we shall hear she is dead.' Yesterday morning M. came into my room—I was still in bed—with your card in her hand and the tears in her eyes. 'Dear Dora is gone,' she said. I cannot say I felt surprised, although death always startles one, and as long as there is life we hope against hope even. But I was glad we had made the Novena, for I felt that our dear Blessed Mother would take the dear child into her loving arms, and folding her to her heart she would receive the blessing of new life either for soul or body. After all, though our tears flow, we can discern, dimly though it may be, a ray of that serene and peaceful light into which she has passed, and in whose fulness is joy for evermore.

"Oh! then, my dear friend, let us thank God for His mercy to us *four*, and let us take courage and go on hopefully to the end, working or waiting or suffering as He shall order, guarding in our hearts the Holy Faith which is His most precious gift, as our dearest treasure, until we come at last, by His grace, to see Him in glory, who is our God in heaven."

Enclosed in my friend's letter was one from her dear child, my beloved goddaughter and Dora's friend.

"My dear, dear godmother," she wrote, "may God give you strength to support with holy resignation this terrible loss. Loss to us, but what a gain to her, our dear Dora, ready for heaven as she was after so much suffering. Think of her, dear Mrs. B., truly happy in heaven with our Lord, our Blessed Lady, and all the Saints. She is indeed to be envied. True it is, she has left us here, but she will pray for us and obtain for us a peaceful happy death like hers, when our hour comes for us to go and join her in those sacred and everlasting joys. Dear Dora was the only young friend whom, I really felt, was always constant and the same. I have no young friends here in A——, and none to whom I could ever attach myself as I did to Dora, but I hope she will still love me in heaven, and pray for me. I thought I was going a short time ago; but no, I was not worthy, and dear Dora was ready before me."

Dora's beloved friend, Fr. L., was not alone in his opinion of her. Another of her " dear Fathers," as she always called them, on hearing of her death thus expressed himself respecting her :—

"I condole with you on the loss of dear Dottie. She was a darling child, so good, so affectionate. You have had moments of anxiety for her, but the anxiety was owing to your affection. Poor Dottie never gave you just reason for anxiety. In her holy death you have the full reward of your more than mother's care for your darling. You have a great loss to deplore, but Dottie has left a world for which she was not fitted, to receive the reward of her sweet innocence. Yes! I will join you in your Te Deum; at the same time I will name the dear child at the Holy Sacrifice. If she does not require our prayers, it will nevertheless please me, and make me more satisfied if I pray for her.—R. I. P.

"Some day, when you have recovered and rested, perhaps when you come to England, you will give me some particulars of Dottie's last days. I am sure that that child could not leave the world without doing and saying much that ought to be remembered. . . . God has made use of you to prepare an angel for heaven ; you lose your angel, but you must be thankful to Him for the task He has assigned you during these last years."

Our much loved and revered Confessor in Rome, as soon as he had received the tidings of the " consoling departure of our beloved Dotty," wrote to me at once "to offer me his sincere

K

congratulations at so happy a termination to her sufferings.

"God in His mercy," he went on to say, "has called her away from this land of sin and misery before she was acquainted with its malice. 'Rapta est, ne malitia mutaret intellectum ejus.' We will offer up our humble prayers for her this evening, and I will offer up the Holy Sacrifice for her to-morrow, according to your intentions and desires. . . . The dear child, I trust, is now in a position to repay you by her prayers for your unbounded love towards her : after God, she owes you everything. . . . I hope you will keep your confidence now, more than ever, in our dear Lord—may His sweet and holy Name be praised for ever."

Even those who had known but little of my child were yet able to appreciate what her loss was to me.

"Oh, my dear Mrs. B.," writes one of these kind friends, "how I feel for you ! I can't do anything but cry with you. Your dear darling . is now in a much happier home ; she will have no more sorrow, no more pain, no more struggles. God, our Heavenly Father, has taken away His own child from this life so full of misery. You were mother, sister, and friend to her, but do not mourn for her as those who have no faith, no hope. Soon, very soon, we shall be with those who have left us. I must go and give a last embrace to the dear, sweet child, and I beg you to let me take some flowers to caress and cover her in her coffin."

One of the most touching of the letters which I received after my darling's death came to me from the mother of a little child, of whom she was "marraine." I give it entire :—

" MADAME,—

"On vous écrit ces quelques lignes pour vous remercier du paquet que vous nous avez envoyé. Et quand nous avons appris que la Marraine de notre petite était morte nous avons eu beaucoup de chagrin Quand on l'a dit à sa filleule elle a beaucoup pleuré, et elle disait, 'ma pauvre marraine est morte, elle est morte pour toujours.' On vous souhaite que Dieu vous garde. Recevez ces sincères salutations.

> "La famille
> "JOUVENAT."

During the two summers which we had passed at Leysin, a lady, who makes every year a sojourn there, was very kind to my child and much interested in her. She was greatly distressed on hearing of her death, and in a letter which she wrote to me immediately after receiving the sad tidings she thus expresses herself:—

"C'est avec bien du chagrin que j'apprends votre triste retour à Aigle avec la dépouille mortelle de votre chère nièce.

"Cette nouvelle bien inattendue à été un coup pour moi, mais si mes regrets sont grands je pense surtout à la perte douloureuse que vous avez faite, et au vide immense que vous devez ressentir.

"J'ai encore devant les yeux l'aimable et gracieuse figure de Mademoiselle Dora, et il me semble en la voyant, impossible qu'elle vous a dit 'Adieu.' Et pourtant, en pensant à cette

nature délicate on sait bien qu'elle n'était pas
faite pour ce monde, mais bien pour se réunir à
ces anges du ciel qui chantent les louanges de
Dieu au-dessus des atteintes du mal et de la
souffrance.

"Elle a tant souffert ici-bas, que pour vous,
chère Madame, ce doit être une consolation que
toutes larmes sont taries de ses yeux."

Of the many who sorrowed over the loss of
my Dora no one felt her passing away more
.deeply than her beloved "Auntie M." who
having herself lost a dear child about a year
before, could better than any one else enter
into my grief.

"I do not know how to write to you *now*,"
she says to *me*, "the end seems to have come
so very suddenly. I feel thankful J.'s note on
Saturday prepared us. . . . Oh, dearest A., is
it not our great comfort that *both* our very dear
ones are taken home, safe home, free from pain
and sin ! What a change for dear Dora, from
suffering and struggling breath to the calm and
rest of Paradise. If we could only realise how
near they are to us, and how close our inter-

course still is with them, surely we should grieve less ; but oh ! the blank their absence leaves. I have thought of you all day, for well I know what you are feeling. The poor children fret sadly. Dora was as one of themselves."

Another of Dora's dearest friends, with whom she had spent many happy hours at the Convent in London, where we had passed four quiet, peaceful months before going abroad, in writing to me of her happy death, and telling me that immediately after receiving my letter she had gone to the chapel and said a Te Deum for her, adds—

" I am certain that dear Dora never lost her baptismal innocence, but went straight to heaven. Her delicacy and suffering only puri-fied her bright soul, and now she is enjoying such happiness as we cannot even con-ceive."

" Poor Dora," her dear " Uncle T." wrote, " she and Mary are once more embracing each other, enjoying the bliss of Paradise, perhaps wondering when we shall join them, and doubt-less praying that one day we may take our happy seats among the blessed company of saints and angels."

Mary had been Dora's dearest child-friend, and very great was her sorrow on hearing of her death, which took place only a few weeks before we left Switzerland, in 1875, on a visit to England. Whilst staying with her "Uncle" and "Aunt" by adoption, Dora said to me, I think two or three nights after our arrival—

"Auntie, I do believe Aunt M. has put me into dear Mary's room, and I think my bed is the one on which she died."

I replied that I could not tell whether it were so or not, but that if she were right and it made her nervous, I was sure her Aunt would gladly give her another room.

"Oh no, no, Auntie," she exclaimed, "do not say anything about it, I would rather stay here. I shall be so glad if this is really Mary's bed; I like to lie here and think of her happy death."

Of course I complied with her request, though I must own her answer astonished me greatly; for Dora had always shown from her earliest childhood a nervous horror of death. She often said she could not bear to think of it, or hear anything about it; whilst to see a dead baby even, would, she fancied, give her a shock from which she would never recover. But our dear Lord and His blessed Mother, little as I then guessed it, were already beginning to prepare her for the end which was even then approaching. She was dwelling with comfort now on dear Mary's last hours, and when to herself the dread summons came she received it with perfect calmness and resignation to the adorable will of God. Recalling afterwards to remembrance the happy weeks spent under their roof her Aunt M. wrote—

"Our house was the last which our beloved Dora visited in England, and we were quite hoping that her first visit on her return this year (1877) would be to us again ; but she is no more in this world, and now we must look to meeting her in a blessed eternity."

A young friend with whom my child and I had become intimate in Rome during the years 1869 and '70, just before we had the happiness of being received into the Catholic Church, says of her :—

" She seemed too good, too precious, too fragile, to be left long in this cold world, though we can ill spare such beautiful examples of innocence from it. My mind will go back night and day to her sweet engaging ways, and to the good she did me in Rome and Lucerne. You may imagine how many tears and regrets are joined to yours."

Not long after my child was taken from me, I wrote to one of the Jesuit Fathers who had seen much of her during the winter of 1873, which we had spent in Rome, asking him to mention any little traits which he might have noticed.

In his reply he says that what struck him most particularly during the time that he knew her, was the maturity of judgment which she displayed, and which was both rare and surprising in so young a girl. He added that she showed it in her conversation in matters respecting the Church, in its doctrines and practices, as well as when speaking on secular subjects.

"She seemed to me," he said, "to be a very devoted Catholic, and most earnest in her convictions as to the truth of the Catholic religion. We certainly have every reason to hope that the dear child has been taken, in her innocence and goodness, to a very happy eternity. She will, no doubt, pray for you and help you, as the good who have gone to their rest can do, so that you may be one day with her amongst the blessed. I shall not easily forget her, so gentle and earnest as she was."

Whilst reading Fr. G.'s letter, it vividly recalled to my recollection a conversation which we had had together in my little salon in the Capo le Case, when speaking of the sweet expression of my child's face, he had said that often in conversing with her he had felt as though she were one of the angels of Fra Angelico's pictures, so exactly did she resemble them in her whole aspect. She made the same impression on others also.

"Votre chère Dora," wrote a friend of ours to me, " ne m'a jamais fait l'effet d'être de ce monde, mais bien un de ces messagers celestes qui passent ici-bas un certain temps pour remplir leur mission et déploient leurs ailes au moment ou le contact avec le monde leur enleverait leur blancheur de lis."

Those, too, who had seen her but seldom seemed always to have borne her in sweet remembrance. An Italian lady who had met her two or three times during our sojourn in Rome, so far back as 1870, remarks in writing of her to a common friend :—

" Tu gia mi aveva scritto della sua morte et mi dispiacque immensamente. Io sempre la rimarcano per la sua simpatia ed affabilita. Ricordo benissimo che un giorno l'incontrai per il Corso dopo averla conosciuta con te ed ella fu la prima a salutarmi. Sarebbe stato meglio che non l'avessi mai conosciuta."

In the spring of 1875 we had spent a few weeks at Montreux. Dora was very ill during part of the time, and had received Holy Communion from a saintly French Abbé who was stationed there. Writing to me after her death he says :—

" Je partage avec vous du plus intime de mon

cœur le chagrin que vous cause la mort de votre bien-aimée Dora. Je lui étais fort attaché, à cause de ses qualités excellentes, aussi je comprends jusqu'à quel point cette séparation vous est douloureuse.

"Mais cette séparation ne sera pas de longue durée, la vie s'écoule vîte, et après quelques jours d'absence, l'on se trouve réunis pour jamais aux êtres chéris que Dieu nous avait prêtés pour charmer un peu notre exil. Et en attendant l'heure de la réunion éternelle dans le sein de notre Père céleste nous pourrons vivre encore en esprit dans la compagnie de ces saintes âmes, qui perdues plus entièrement dans l'essence divine se trouvent ainsi plus rapprochées de nous. Elles nous voient, elles prient pour nous, et se préparent à nous recevoir bientôt dans leur sainte et glorieuse société.

"Je me suis empressé d'offrir le Saint Sacrifice à l'intention de votre chère enfant, non que je pense qu'elle en ait besoin, car son purgatoire a été long et rude en cette pauvre vie, mais l'oblation de l'auguste sacrifice sera alors utile à nous-mêmes."

"After all," wrote one, who although she had never seen Dora, had heard enough of her to feel deeply interested in everything respecting her, "we who have lived long, and have experienced what deep and terrible affliction life can bring, especially to women, should not mourn for one who has been early removed to a happier life than this can ever be. Your beloved child, I heard yesterday from Mrs. M., was 'very clever,' and it is, I think, those who are the most gifted who suffer the most in the battle of life. . . . . Thank you much for sending me a photograph of your Dora; what a sweet, thoughtful face it is! I had a letter from my sister-in-law yesterday: speaking of you, she says, 'I thought her Dora such a dear little thing.' I so well understand your not liking to leave her (as it seems to us) behind you at Aigle when you return home. There is not one of all the heartrending trials we are bid to endure greater than this one. People say this is only sentiment, but *that* does not lessen the pang. . . . . Your Dora will be often prayed for in that dear little chapel, the best place in Aigle."

"I heard that your beloved child was very clever." Yes, that was the impression she made on all who saw her, and yet she was so modest and retiring that it was only those who knew her well who could rightly appreciate her many and brilliant gifts. She had amongst them a surprising talent for languages. When we were in Rome in 1869 she learnt—I cannot tell how —to speak Italian with such fluency that no one, unknowing who she was, took her for an English child, but seeing her fair hair and complexion, often used to ask whether she were a Florentine. One of the prelates of Rome, Mgr. N., no mean judge, assured me that it was impossible for even a native to speak with greater accuracy or a purer accent, and he added that the most surprising part was she could speak the language of the people with as much ease as she could that of the educated classes. French, also, she spoke with almost equal fluency, but she had not the same affection for it as for the melodious Italian tongue, which, with the people and the country, she so dearly loved.

From her childhood she had been fond of Art,

and during her stay in Rome our visits to its galleries so educated her eye and her taste, that no second-rate productions had afterwards any power to please her. Fr. G. once told me that he was surprised at the appreciation she showed of paintings by the old masters, and at her always choosing the highest and best works as objects for her admiration. For drawing she showed remarkable talent, and had her life been prolonged, it would have been her favourite pursuit. She was very clever with her fingers, and often delighted to surprise me with some of her little contrivances and inventions.

As regards her character, the story I have given of her last days has, I trust, brought out its most salient and beautiful features. But I must here mention that before Dora became a Catholic, and during the earlier years of her life, she had given me some trouble and anxiety. She had a very strong will, and it was often not without a painful contest that she could bring herself to submit to mine. She was also at times somewhat perverse and dictatorial, as well as fond of arguing over everything she was desired to do, and she gave way at times to what looked very like impertinence, though I do not think she ever meant it to be so. After her conversion, however, all these faults were gradually subdued, until during the latter portion of her life they entirely faded away, and were superseded by the fruits of the Spirit—"charity, peace, patience, benignity, goodness, longanimity, mildness, faith, modesty, chastity;"—none of these lovely qualities were wanting, and they all attained to greater ripeness and maturity each succeeding year, until the end came and they were perfected.

She had always been a very imaginative child, and I remember that when she was not more than seven years old and had no companions of her own age, I used to see her walking up and down our garden, busily talking, and then pausing, as though listening to the answer of an invisible person. I asked her one day what it all meant. At first she would give me no answer; then she said she had two pretended companions, one of whom was called "Jane" and the other "Sarah." Jane was very good, and she liked her very much; but Sarah was naughty, and was always wanting her to do wrong things—and that was the reason why she was so often naughty. After that time, whenever she was particularly good, I found, on questioning her, that she had been talking to Jane; and whenever she was specially naughty, that Sarah had been telling her things which she would repeat to me with as much detail and in as matter-of-fact a way as though the conversation had really taken place between them. She never gave any one the impression of being a very thoughtful child, and yet I am sure she was, as was evident from the startling things she used every now and then to say. For example : I was one day speaking to her of everlasting death, and trying as well as I could to explain it to her. "It is very awful, Auntie," she remarked, "but I think everlasting life is quite as awful. I do not like to think about it, do you?" She often said very witty things, which would bring a smile to my lips even during her illness, and up to the last she was always gay and bright.

I do not think I ever met with any one who had a clearer and deeper insight into character than she possessed, or who had a greater horror and detestation of "shams" of all kinds. Truth was the guiding principle of her life ; it was the first quality for which she looked in the characters of those with whom she was brought in contact, and I sometimes told her, she was too severe in her condemnation when she met with any lack of it in persons who, through timidity or nervousness, deviated ever so slightly from accuracy in speech or action. Her judgment was seldom at fault, and in difficult circumstances she would frequently give me the good, sensible advice which I had sought in vain from persons older and more experienced than herself. And yet with it all she was most childlike and most diffident, especially in matters regarding herself, which she was never content to decide, without first making an appeal to me and obtaining my opinion. She had a keen sense of the ridiculous, and her powers of mimicry were something extraordinary.. In the visits we were wont to pay during our sojourns in Rome to one of the prelates, with whom "dear Dottie," as he used to call her, was an especial favourite, nothing used to delight him more than her imitations of some of the droll characters, to be met with every day in Rome. It was surprising that she was not quite spoilt by the admiration she excited everywhere; but it seemed as though hers was a nature which could not be spoilt; and it must not be forgotten that her religion preserved her from many of the temptations to which she would otherwise have yielded, added to which she seemed to me always to consider admiration as being but another name for love.

Up to the time when she became a Catholic, I had always looked upon her as an unusually sceptical and incredulous child, but from that date not a doubt ever seemed to cross her mind. She had attained a haven of rest, and was completely. satisfied. Her faith, as those who had the best opportunities of judging unite in saying, was something wonderful, and her devotion to the Blessed Virgin most entire and touching. Whenever she wished or hoped for anything, it was to her she instinctively went, nor had she ever the slightest doubt about her petitions being answered, even though, as she often used to say, "they might not be answered as soon, or in the way which she expected." Her trust, too, in the power of the Saints to help her, and her certainty in the efficacy of their intercessions, was very striking and beautiful; and she carried it into the most trivial details of her daily life.

"I looked for such and such a thing everywhere," she would say, "but I should never have found it if it had not been for S. Antony." "Now, that is S. Joseph's doing," she would exclaim, when anything pleasant—which, perhaps, she had long wished and prayed for—happened. "You know Fr. L. always said he was the most good-natured saint he knew," she would smilingly remark. Yet she was never superstitious, and used unmercifully to ridicule all belief in "omens, dreams, and such like fooleries," a passage she was fond of quoting from the Catechism.

The Catholic faith was so firmly rooted in her heart, that she found it increasingly difficult to comprehend how any one could remain a Protestant after having become acquainted with its doctrines.

"Oh, if they would only give it a month's trial, like we give servants sometimes," she used to say, " I am sure, Auntie, that they could not be anything but Catholics afterwards. It is just because they don't know anything about it that they remain Protestants."

This, too, was her great comfort when thinking of dear friends and relatives still wandering outside the fold. "Lord, forgive them, for they know not what they do," was ever the spirit of her intercessory prayers on their behalf. At the same time she could not understand how it was that, after reading all that is said of our Blessed Lady in their Bibles, Protestants should still continue to hold her in such slight esteem, and show her so little affection.

" They know how delightful it is to have a mother on earth," she would say, "why do they object so much to having a mother in heaven ? They call Jesus Christ their brother, and yet they will not call His mother their mother. It is very strange, isn't it? If they loved Him as Catholics do, they could not help loving His mother also."

She always hailed with the greatest delight any, the slightest sign of *rapprochement*, to the Catholic Church on the part of those she loved, and was always sensitively afraid lest by unconsidered words or incautious deeds she should quench the smoking flax, and so repel from, rather than attract, those whom she loved to that blessed fold where she had herself found rest, peace, and happiness untold. Yet, if she were drawn into an argument, I used to be astonished at her powers of reasoning, the logical manner in which she treated every objection raised, the clearness of her statements, and the moderation she always displayed. It might, indeed, be said of her, that she combined the wisdom and insight of a person of mature years, with the simplicity and modesty of a child.

A most devoted and earnest Catholic my Dora indeed was. She loved our Holy Father Pope Pius IX. with all the enthusiasm of her ardent nature, and delighted to speak of the favours which she had received at his hands. Chief amongst these was a medal he had sent to her on the occasion of making her first Communion in the Convent of St. M. I had written to our revered Confessor, Mgr. K., in Rome, telling him of the day on which it was to take place—the Epiphany—and begging his prayers for his dear child in Christ. He chanced to be going to the Vatican on the day when my letter arrived, and mentioning its contents to the Holy Father, entreated him to send his blessing to Dora. Pius IX. well remembered the golden-haired, sweet-looking English child, to whom he had addressed, in our audiences of him at the Vatican, many affectionate and never-to-be-forgotten words. After acceding to Mgr. K.'s request, he went into his bedroom, and returning thence in a few moments, put a medal into Mgr.'s hands, desiring him to send it to Dora "as a remembrance of the great mercy which our loving Redeemer would confer upon her on the happy day of her first Communion, and of the ardent solicitude of His Vicar for her eternal salvation."

I will not attempt to describe the joy which
this precious gift, and the message which accom-
panied it, gave to her. "Am I not a spoilt
child, Auntie?" she would say. "Was there
ever any one so happy as I am?"

What intense pleasure, too, did it give her to
call up bright visions of a future—destined, alas!
never to be realised—when the beloved Holy
Father would be restored to his own again, and
Rome become once more, as of old, the Holy
City. "Oh! to be there then," she would exclaim, "it would be too much happiness. I
think I should cry myself away with joy."

She had first seen Rome when it was at the
height of its glory, during the winter of the
years 1869-70, whilst the Council of the Vatican
was being held, and all the great services of the
Church were being celebrated with unusual
splendour and solemnity. Of course the impression made upon her susceptible nature was
very deep, and it was rendered all the more so
by the contrast which everywhere met her sight
when we revisited Rome the succeeding winter.
Her indignation at all she saw and heard was

very great, and she manifested it on every possible occasion with the utmost fearlessness. Some short prayers had been given her for distribution, and she was very fond of presenting them to the soldiers, to whom, in her voluble Italian, she would explain their meaning, and exhort them to use them. She made her little offerings in such a smiling, sweet manner that she never met with a rebuff; on the contrary, she often succeeded in gaining the confidence of those to whom she spoke, and finding to her joy that they entirely entered into and shared all her feelings with regard to the changes which had taken place.

She had a great love of reading. History was her favourite study; and she always took intense interest in anything that had reference to the French Revolution. For novels of the present day she cared little, but she delighted in tales of chivalry. Her eye would kindle, her cheeks flush, and her lips tremble, whilst listening to the recital of some noble or heroic deed, or of passages in the lives of our English Catholic forefathers and martyrs for the faith.

I had accustomed her from childhood to consult me as to her choice of books, and never
allowed her to read any which had been lent to
her until she had first shown them to me.
Latterly, when I told her she was becoming old
enough to choose sometimes for herself, she was
never satisfied or happy until she had my opinion
or approval, and this habit remained with her to
the last. If, as in the case of "The Home of
the Lost Child," books were given to her by a
person on whom I felt I could depend—though
in that instance, unfortunately, I was mistaken—
I left it to her to read them without asking me
to look over them first, but almost invariably
she brought them to me. Once I remember
she got a book from the library which she had
selected because of its attractive title only, and
asked me whether she might read it. I answered
Yes, and she took the book away. It was an
exciting story, and she told me she was delighted
with it so far as she had read. The next day I
suddenly remembered that towards the end it
contained some passages which were very objec-
tionable, and, telling her so, I asked her to read

no more. She looked disappointed, but after exclaiming " Oh, Auntie, what a pity !" she at once closed the book and sent it back to the library.

For poetry her taste had hardly yet been cultivated, but she would listen with entranced pleasure to passages which I read to her from Tennyson, and specially from " The Idylls of the King."

Once a young friend of hers had requested her to write "answers" to a book of questions such as used to be formerly more in vogue than they are at present. It was only with great reluctance she consented, for she was so afraid of being unconsciously untruthful ; but at last she gave way. Her answers, as I afterwards felt, were a faithful picture of herself. Thus her favourite virtues, she wrote, were truth and unselfishness ; her favourite qualities in men, firmness and gentleness, and in women, self-sacrifice. The occupation in which she took most pleasure was cookery ; her chief characteristic, she said, was contrariness ; her idea of happiness, poor child, was " never to take cold ;"

her idea of misery, "wearing rough woollen
stockings." If not herself, she would rather be
a Sister of Charity; roses were the flowers she
liked best; Raphael and Mozart her favourite
painter and composer; St. Sebastian, St. Agnes,
and Mary Stuart her favourite heroines in real
life, Fabiola and Enid in fiction. Her pet aver-
sion was a squeaking door, her favourite food
bread and butter. Telling a lie to save the life
of another was the sin for which she thought
she should have most toleration. " Fais ce que
tu dois, advienne que pourra," was the motto
she would choose.

For everything that was beautiful and refined
she had the highest appreciation, but it was not
until we went to Italy that her love for scenery
became thoroughly developed and expanded.
From that time forth, the Roman Campagna,
the Alban and Sabine Hills, the view from the
heights of Florence of the plain of the Arno,
were the standard of beauty from which she
never departed until the last few months of her
life, when the lakes and mountains of Switzerland
seemed almost to usurp the place which had

hitherto been occupied by her recollections of
Italy.

From her earliest infancy she had been a very
sweet-looking and attractive child. On the
occasion of our first visit to Rome people often
used to address her as we were walking through
the streets as one of Christ's little angels, and
passing their hands through her fair locks would
exclaim "seta d'oro," or say that the sunshine
had become entangled in her hair. By our
Italian servants she was passionately loved, and
all the more so because of the lively interest she
always showed in their family affairs, making
herself in every way one of them, than which
there is no surer means of finding one's way to
Italian hearts. I do not think any child was
ever more laden with gifts than she was during
the whole course of her life. "How good and
kind every one is to me," she would often say ;
and even during her last illness it was an
expression which over and over again would
cross her lips.

Ah ! when I recall to mind all that my Dora
was, and thereby become, if possible, more and

more sensible of my loss, it is impossible that I should not also feel how merciful God has been in taking her thus early to Himself, as being indeed one of those of whom this world is not worthy. Very merciful too was the dispensation which removed her before my summons came.

"Try to think of the reverse of the picture," a dear friend wrote to me, "you lying dead, and she gazing upon you. Would you not do anything to save her from *that?*"

We were, in truth, so entirely one that had I been taken, life would indeed have been desolate and hard for her.

"I never can forget you and your child," the wife of an English clergyman said to me, "neither can I ever think of the one without remembering the other."

"Think what would have been dear Dottie's life," writes another beloved friend, "if she had survived you ; she so dearly cared for, so lovingly cherished, with her precarious health needing a fostering watchfulness, which there was no one to give her in this world as you did. Think of this, which might readily have been in your weak state, and be not only resigned but *happy* that she is safe with God."

I have spoken of the impression my child made upon even those with whom she had little more than a passing acquaintanceship. A touching proof lies before me in a letter from a lady who was staying at a mountain hotel where we spent some days the year before Dora's death.

"Thank you very much," she says in a letter written to me some months ago, "for giving me some particulars of the peaceful going home of your dearest child. She was so sweet and gentle, patient and unselfish; I always regretted seeing so little of her, and indeed from the depths of my heart I sympathise with you and grieve with you for your loss."

Another lady, who only saw her once, said to me not long ago—

"I shall never forget that one visit your Dora paid me, nor what an angel she looked; the recollection of the sweetness and modesty of her manner, her bright animated smile, and the affection which shone in her eyes whenever she looked at or addressed her Auntie, are recollections which will remain with me always."

"I dare not write to you about what has happened," wrote a friend who had seen Dora two or three times whilst we were in London in 1873. "I cannot think of it without tears. She was so young and sweet and childlike that an idea of my own children mixes itself up with Dora whenever I think of it, and I find myself crying over the thought of *that*, and of what you are feeling. There are comforts in your religion denied to ours. I trust you feel something of them. I know you do, and hope time will heal the wound."

By young and old, high and low, by the learned and unlearned, my child had been equally and deeply loved during her sweet life, and by them all she was alike and deeply regretted after her death.

"Dear Mrs. B.," a little protégée of hers wrote to me, "I was so sorry to hear of Miss Dora's death. I little thought when I was writing to her that she would not open my letter. I wish I could have seen her before she died, but God thought it was better for me not to see her. I received your letter on the 25th of August. I did not think of the sad, sad news inside, and I could not help but cry, it seemed so hard to have such a kind, loving friend taken away. But she has gone to Heaven, where we all hope to go when we die, and where she will feel no more pain or sorrow. I was so pleased with the photographs you sent me of dear Miss Dora, and the other of the châlet where she died. I shall always keep them in remembrance of her. I did so love her, and I know she loved me. I was always thinking of her; but, dear Mrs. B., you will be my friend now Miss Dora has gone; and will you please write to me often, for I shall want to hear from you."

I cannot refrain from citing, as a beautiful proof of the love borne to my child by all with whom she came in contact, a letter written to me by one of whose friendship she was most justly proud, and which she ever regarded as indeed her "title of honour." From the time when he first saw her, a little child, with, as he said, "the face of a angel," until she passed

M

away, he had always taken the most lively and affectionate interest in her welfare, and great was the regret which her death occasioned him.

"It was indeed kind of you," he said, " to make known to me from yourself the cropping of this flower, which you have tended with such deep and constant affection, and which is now taken in all its purity to bloom in the better land. I cannot be sorry for her sake that she is added to the company of the just, gone—
   'To where beyond these voices there is peace ;'
for the din of earthly strife waxes louder and more wearying from year to year, and it was much too rude a climate and too harsh a scene for her. As for me, I need not assure you that I have remembered her before God this day, at the most solemn hour, and pray that His abundant rest, light, and peace may be multiplied upon her. I feel for your bereavement, but doubtless you will be sustained under it, and you will find a prop and consolation in the memories of your offices towards her. She will help to carry you across the stream where you will see—

' Those angel faces smile
Which we have loved long since and lost awhile.' "

There is still a letter amongst the innumerable
ones which I received after my darling left me
for Paradise, which I must indulge myself in the
pleasure of adding to those from which I have
already quoted so largely, and which were the
means, under God, of imparting to me much
strength and consolation in those first sad hours
of anguish and desolation. It is from the
revered and venerated head of the Catholic
hierarchy in England, to whom I had taken my
child on the eve of our departure for the Conti-
nent in 1873, that she might receive his bene-
diction.

"Your letter of sad tidings," he says, "has
never been off my table since it reached me.
. . . . I feared that the day which has come at
last could not be long delayed. But you have
more than consolation. You may rejoice in the
confidence that our Lord had marked out that
good child for His own. To you it must be a
great and hourly loss, which nothing can fill up,
But we must look onward and upward, not

downward or back upon the past. The love of
our Divine Lord does all things for us, and if
we trust Him fully He will never fail to give us
strength and consolation for every day.

" May God be with you."

Yes ! great indeed were my consolations, and
not amongst the least of them were the tributes
of affection shown to me, not only in letters and
at her funeral, but in the remembrance of her
shown by the flowers laid from time to time
upon her grave. More than a year has now
elapsed since she was laid at rest, and when
the first anniversary of her passing away
arrived, it was not forgotten. I was away from
Aigle at the time, but in my far-off exile I was
not left without many touching proofs of the
manner in which my Dora was still held in
affectionate recollection. I had sent to a young
girl-friend of hers a cross of immortelles to be
laid on the grave, and soon afterwards I received from her the following letter :—

"Ce matin déjà, j'ai reçu la croix d'immortelles ; elle est tout à fait intacte, et pas une
fleur n'est tombée. Après midi je suis allée au

cimetière et nous avons tout orné, Marguerite et moi, la tombe de notre bien-aimée Dora ; du reste déjà couverte de fleurs. Devant, il y avait un jacinthe blanche, et une lilas près du marbre ; puis une cinéraire au milieu, et après cette plante deux primevères, une blanche et une rose. Des guirlandes de mousse couvraient la terre et étaient tout à fait remplies de perce-neiges et de violettes. Derrière enfin, il y avait des immortelles. J'ai mis la croix devant le marbre, entre les deux jacinthes, et nous avons complètement garni la barrière avec du laurier teint en sorte qu'il n'y a pas une place libre même par terre. Pensant que cela vous ferait sans doute plaisir d'avoir une ou deux fleurs du tombeau de Dora j'en ai mis quelques-unes dans une petite boîte, et j'espère qu'elles vous arriveront pas trop gatées.

" Chère Madame, cette journée a dû être bien triste pour vous. Je vous assure que nous avons bien parlé de vous, et que nos cœurs vous suivaient là-bas puisque nous ne pourrions pas vous voir. À nous aussi, et à moi surtout, cela nous a fait bien de la peine de penser à cette chère Dora, et je vous assure qu'en arrangeant la tombe, j'avais le cœur bien, bien gros.

"Enfin, elle est maintenant heureuse, et bien plus heureuse que nous. Marguerite était très émue, et me disait que Dora voyait peutêtre les fleurs dont sa tombe était couverte; et que comme elle aimait le bon Dieu, elle devait être très heureuse."

The dear young friend who had thus covered her grave with flowers, also wrote to me, saying—

"You may be sure we thought of you much yesterday, and of dear little Dora. I went quite early in the morning, and covered her last resting-place with flowers. . . . It has been a sweet work of love to me, for your sake and for hers. I have been so fond of going to her grave when I have felt sad. It reminded me that I was not the only one who had heavy sorrows to bear."

"Especially have I been thinking of you," wrote another kind friend, "on this first anniversary of so much sorrow to you, but, as you say, of such happiness and bliss to your dear Dora. I was much touched the other day on opening a book I have not read for years, to find within it a translation, in the dear child's writing, done in the ladies' little salon of our hotel at Lucerne. At least her present happiness and her being taken away from the troubles of this world must be some comfort for you, although I am sure that her loss is irreparable."

"How does dear Dora's grave look now?" asked her especial friend E. "I should like to send you some of my lilies for it. Dear Dora! she was like a lily of the valley herself."

"I hardly believe in the increased sorrow of *early* anniversaries," was the observation made by a beloved friend, in a letter written to me at this time ; "but I can scarcely tell, so many phases has grief. Yet in the first weeks or months, or even years, during which the silence of the beloved voice, the absence of the loving looks, tell us that the being so dear has left us for ever, the wounds of the heart bleed as at the first moment of the dread loss. As time passes on, and with its healing power softens the blow, anniversaries *do* renew the first bitterness of grief, and we seem to live over and over again

all that we then endured. A year back, and
how sweet and pure must your darling have
looked in that unbroken sleep which brought
her rest, unbroken indeed here, but what an
awakening !

"I wish I had seen her again, dear child ! My
poor Dottie ! I too loved her dearly. I wish
I could have done her or you any good !

"Ah ! my dear, dear friend, shall we ever
know in this world the good she has done to
us both, and for which she has received an
exceeding great reward ?"

One more letter I must quote : it is from the
lady who had been so kind to my Dora during
our sojourns at Leysin, and who has proved
since her death so dear a friend to myself.

"J'ai bien pensé à vous à Noël," she says, "et
au commencement de l'année, ne me doutant
pas cependant que vous passiez ces fêtes dans
votre lit. Et maintenant le temps vous rap-
proche d'une date qui a pour vous des souvenirs
bien amères et bien durs. Puisse la paix qui a
rendu si calme les derniers moments de votre
enfant descendre aussi sur vous, et vous mettre

en communion avec le monde invisible, comme
cela est arrivé à l'heure de l'agonie de celle que
vous pleurez. . . . . La description que vous
me faites de ce palmier magnifique que vous
avez en face de votre fenêtre, et de la belle
végétation qui vous entoure me donnerait grand
envie d'aller vous rejoindre, mais hélas ! je suis
rivée à Aigle, et il faut bien en prendre mon
parti.

" Mais j'en reviens sans cesse à votre palmier,
comprenant le langage qu'il vous parle, et heureuse de sentir ce que vous dit la Nature, et les
pensées qu'éveille en vous cet arbre symbolique,
tout en élévant votre cœur envers les régions
célestes. . . . De là, à votre ange il n'y a qu'un
élan, et cette pensée doit augmenter la paix de
votre âme, puisque vous savez qu'elle est dans la
lumière, et qu'en vous attendant elle est heureuse auprès de son Sauveur. *Aimer et croire,*
tout est là, et si les larmes coulent dans la terre
d'exil, on sait pourtant qu'un jour viendra où ils
seront essuyées. En pensant à vos tristesses, à
votre solitude comparative, je pense souvent à
ce revoir qui vous attend et au bonheur que

vous avez de le savoir et d'avoir vu votre chère enfant déployer ses ailes d'ange en quittant un monde de péché. C'est un grand privilége, et un cœur aimant comme le votre doit le sentir lorsque l'âme souffre de la séparation."

Ah, yes ! it is a great privilege to be able to look forward with a sure and certain hope to the day when those who have been parted on earth shall once more meet in Heaven ; a great and precious privilege to have beheld such a calm and sweet and holy passing away as that of my beloved child. Meet it was that all who loved her should join with their " De Profundis" a "Te Deum" for her happy flight ; a " Te Deum" to which we have every reason to believe that she, with the angels, responded. Her death has indeed been one of the heaviest trials of my life, and yet tears of thankful joy will ever mingle with those which are grief-laden whenever I recall to mind the great grace which our dear Lord accorded her in permitting her to breathe out her soul in " perfect peace."

God grant that the like happy end may be in store for all the dear friends who may read this imperfect story of my Dora's last days, and that her young friends especially may be led by it to endeavour to imitate her saintly innocent life in order that, like her, they may obtain the crowning grace of a holy, peaceful death.

* * * * *

It was only a few days after writing these last words that I received a note from the dear friend from whose letters I have already made so many quotations, and to which I cannot choose but add yet another extract. She says :—

"Je suis bien contente, chère Madame, que vous avez achevé votre ouvrage à la mémoire de Mlle. Dora. Je ne doute pas que quoique absente elle ne puisse, grâce à vous, faire encore du bien à plusieurs dans ce monde, même à ceux qui ne l'ont pas connue. Pour nous qui avons été frappés de l'expression de son pur regard, nous avons compris que sous sa frêle envelope se cachait une belle âme, et que le pur rayonnement de ses yeux était un reflet du ciel.

"Cela explique aussi le sourire qui errait sur ses levres lorsque en proie à la souffrance ou à

l'oppression elle vous disait si tranquillement,
' Ah, je ne suis pas très bien aujourd'hui.' Le
ciel pour elle était rapproché, elle le portait dans
son cœur, grâce à sa Communion constante avec
le Dieu invisible : Voilà pourquoi on se sentait
attiré vers elle, pourquoi on avait la tentation de
se retourner lorsqu'elle avait passé, et pourquoi
aussi, lorsqu'elle avait une vérité pénible à dire
c'était avec cette conviction et cette force
qu'on trouve chez les fortes natures et rare-
ment chez les natures délicates secouèes par
les vents de l'affliction. Dieu était là, on le
sentait, et quoique morte, elle le dit encore."

And now that my labour of undying love and
sorrowful regret is over, what more can I add?
Nothing ; excepting that, spite of my own endur-
ing grief for the loss of so dear a child, I am
quite sure that all I have suffered for God's sake
in yielding her up to Him will seem as nothing
when I enter into eternity, and there behold all
my past life. Then with the saints I shall be
ready to wish for another existence in which to
suffer something more for my dear Lord and
Saviour.

" Oh, my Saviour, Thou who hast suffered for my sake all the torments of Thy Passion, even to the most cruel death of the Cross, I do not refuse, whatever it may cost me, to take part in Thy bitter cup. I offer to Thee my heart, torn but resigned. Thou hast given me in this child, so tenderly beloved, the sweetest happiness my life has ever known. I submit, in so far as it is possible for me in my desolation, to the decree whereby Thou hast taken her from me. Yes, my God, my Creator, the Ruler of all things, I desire with Thy servant Job to bless Thy holy Name in this terrible trial, and to abandon myself without reserve to Thy most holy Will, which never can be cruel. Oh, my Consoler, Thou wilt not condemn my tears, Thou who didst weep over the death of Thy friend Lazarus. Only do not Thou permit one single word to pass my lips, or one feeling to rise in my heart, which may be in any way displeasing to Thee. And grant that I may not indulge in a single thought which is not in conformity with the absolute and Christian submission which I owe to Thee. Oh, my God, grant that my grief may never be mingled with despair, that I may never give myself up to it at the expense of my duties, and that the regret I feel for the child I have lost may never render me unjust to the dear ones who still remain to me. Give me the power to be always solicitous for their happiness, vigilant in controlling myself when grief is attempting to take possession of my heart, and courageous in raising up my stricken soul from the dust in which it would fain lie."

" Blessed Virgin, Mother of Dolours, I unite my sufferings with thine ; open to me thy heart, the refuge and the pattern of desolate mothers : obtain for me, O Mary! by thy prayers, that I may accept like Thee the sword which has pierced my soul ; that I may remain *standing* at the foot of the Cross, that I may live there, and that there I may die, submissive and resigned. Amen. Alleluia ! Alleluia !"*

---

* L.'Abbé Legris-Duval.

THE END.

www.ingramcontent.com/pod-product-compliance
Lightning Source LLC
Chambersburg PA
CBHW020002030726
47500CB00002B/398